News at Eleven
A Novel

Doris Gaines Rapp

News at Eleven
A Novel

Doris Gaines Rapp

Daniel's House Publishing

Copyright © 2015 by Doris Gaines Rapp

Daniel's House Publishing
P.O. BOX 623
Huntington, Indiana 46750

This book is a work of fiction. Names, characters, places and incidents are either products of the author's imagination or used fictitiously. Any resemblance to actual events, locales or persons, living or dead, is entirely coincidental.

All rights reserved, including the right to reproduce this book or portions thereof in any form whatsoever.

For information contact:
Daniel's House Publishing
P.O. Box 623
Huntington, Indiana 46750
www.danielshousepublishing@gmail.com

Cover design © Debi Lindhorst/The Type Galley
photo of Studio On Air © On-Air/Thinkstock
photo of woman © Oleg Gekman/Thinkstock

Library of Congress Control Number: 2015904624

ISBN: 978-0-9915033-7-7 (paperback)

ISBN: 978-0-9915033-8-4 (eBook)

Table of Contents

Dedication

This book is dedicated to all those who read my novelette, *News at Eleven* in Glo Magazine during January, February, March, and April - 2015. I knew there was more to Clisty Sinclair's story and I knew you would want to know what happened to Faith Sterling. Your eagerness to share Clisty's journey with others, as you passed Glo around to family and friends, inspired me to expand it into a novel. Thank you so much for your enthusiastic interest!

Acknowledgements

A huge thank you to **Melissa Long**, 21Alive TV news anchor of the weekday 5 pm, 6 pm and 11 pm newscasts. She is a busy woman, chosen "Fort Wayne's Favorite TV Personality" ten times by readers of "Whatzup" magazine, and "Best TV Anchor" in the Journal Gazette Reader's Poll. Yet, she took time to read *News at Eleven - A Novel* and wrote an endorsement for the back cover. You can see why Fort Wayne, Indiana residents love her.

A really big thank you to **Glo Magazine**, A Publication of The Papers Incorporated. In September 2014, Betsy Didier passed my name on to the editor of Glo, as an author for the 2015 Glo novelette. I was thrilled! Thank you for the opportunity to share Clisty Sinclair, the news anchor in *New at Eleven*, with your readers. That novelette grew into *News at Eleven – A Novel* because of the interest of your readers!

Thanks to **Debi Lindhorst**, at The Type Galley in Warren, Indiana for her talent in creating the cover. I know what a cover should look like when it's done but have no idea how to get it that way. She does! typegalley@gmail.com

My photograph on the back cover is by **Bonnie Tobey Manning**: website —www.printroom.com/pro/btmanning. Thanks Bonnie!

Prologue

Clisty Sinclair had thought about her childhood friend, Faith Sterling, every day since they were both nine years old. Eighteen years ago, Faith vanished. In every crowd, at every mall, Clisty searched each face for her friend. *I wonder if she's here.* She never was, but Clisty's eyes never stopped searching and her heart never stopped hoping. *Maybe I'll find Faith today?*

Part I
News at Eleven - 1

Clisty Sinclair froze as she stared into the monitor. *It can't be her. It's been too long.*

The television camera zoomed in as Clisty's eyes filled with tears. Shaken, she was numb to the fact that viewers were watching her relive a terrible memory.

The news director's expression widened. "Go on!" she mouthed.

Clisty felt nine years old again, frantically grabbing her friend's hand. But, in the desperate tug-of-war with evil, the muscular man won and dragged her friend away.

She composed herself. "Help police find the witness visible on the ATM's surveillance camera," she reported. "Call 555-2020. Let's roll that again." Clisty stopped breathing as she watched the jerky video. A huge figure in dark clothes ran from the bank, nearly knocking down a disheveled woman. The woman paid no attention to him, but focused on the ATM. At the surveillance camera, she looked directly into it with guarded, anxious eyes.

"Those eyes," Clisty murmured.

Dan Drummond, the senior anchor, waited as Clisty remained silent. Finally Drummond intervened. "Well, that's the news from the Fort. WFT-TV ... Fort Wayne, Indiana. More news at eleven."

"Good show, people." Rebecca Landers waved her arms in the air. "Everything all right?" she asked Clisty.

"Sure Becca." But, she muttered, "It can't be her."

"Who?" Becca jerked the headset from her ears and handed it to her assistant. "Here, George, stow these until eleven, please."

"No one. Just my imagination," Clisty whispered then changed the subject. "Maybe they'll find that witness in time for the eleven o'clock news."

"Maybe, but that's only four hours from now. It could happen, if she walks into police headquarters by herself," Becca answered. "What happened up there?"

"Nothing," she brushed the question off.

"Don't forget the envelope for Clisty." George put the headset on the desk. "I'm going to run out. I'll be back."

"What envelope?" Clisty asked as she stood up slowly.

"Fellow said his name was Phil and left it for you," George called over his shoulder.

"You're slowing down. Are you okay? I'll call a stand-in."

"No, Becca, don't do that. I don't want someone else to look good. I still have to prove myself." She had risen from intern, to fill-in, to junior-anchor in record time. "I don't want anyone to think they made a mistake in hiring me."

"Okay, but you need to talk about it."

"George said you have a letter for me?" Clisty asked.

Becca withdrew the message from her hip pocket. "Here ya go. Hope I didn't wrinkle it."

Clisty pushed dark blond hair from her forehead and studied the envelope. The handwriting looked familiar and yet not. "There's a pot of coffee at my apartment. Can you run out with me for a while? I think I'd better eat something. I'm shaking."

"Sure. We have nothing until eleven."

• • • • •

"Looks like you painted last weekend," Becca observed as she walked around Clisty's living room. "It's still white though isn't it?"

"No. It's cream," Clisty insisted.

"Cream?" Becca said with a wry smile. "Maybe off-white ... but, not cream." She studied the pictures clustered above the sofa. "The girl on the right looks like you." The gangly girl in the photo had skinned knees that stuck out below pale blue summer shorts. Play equipment in the background revealed an active child.

"It is," Clisty agreed. She placed the envelope on the shiny black coffee table. "I'll get us some coffee and yogurt." She walked over to the open kitchen.

"That's great. It's Jason's poker night. He'll stop at the drive-through." She glanced back at the picture, then around Clisty's space. "I'm surprised you hung that picture in a room with white walls." Becca raised her eyebrows. "Sorry, cream walls, white area rug." She looked down. "I know I was right that time, cream sofa and side chairs, and end tables with absolutely nothing on them, no tchotchkes, nothing." She looked again at the fireplace. "I take that back. There's a little angel on the mantle."

"That's my prayer angel. At church, Grandma picked my angel and I got hers that Christmas before she and Grandpa moved to Florida." She smiled defiantly. "Besides, no-clutter settles the mind and makes my space manageable."

"You don't strike me as a control freak."

"I'm not." Clisty removed her shoes, sat cross-legged on the sofa and pealed the lid from the raspberry yogurt. She put it on the saucer.

Becca watched and did the same, except for the leg position. "You could fool me," Becca mused as she glanced around the spotless room. "You take minimalism to an extreme not often seen."

"It's just my home that has to be sterile." She scooped out a spoonful of the creamy treat. "Don't laugh. I don't know why, but my house must be stripped of all clutter."

"You know ... one person's clutter ..." Becca sighed as she sipped the hot coffee. She sat the cup on its saucer and glanced at the envelope.

"Has it grown larger than the room?" Clisty teased as she watched Becca's expression.

"I don't know why you're not interested in what's inside!"

"Oh okay," she chuckled softly. "But, it was fun for a few minutes. I watched your curiosity rise to hyperventilation level."

"Open it!" Becca yelled.

"All right, all right," Clisty drew out slowly. Once opened, the envelope appeared to be empty. She shook it and a square piece of plastic fell out. Pent-up grief crossed her face. She frantically snatched up the piece from the polished floor.

"What is it?"

"It's a four-leaf clover, sealed between clear contact-paper." She held the piece between her index finger and thumb. "My mother lines her closet shelves with clear contact."

"But Clisty," Becca stared at her. "What does it mean? You recognize it. I can tell."

Clisty gently lifted the photo from the wall. "The other sweet child is Faith. She was my dearest friend. We investigated everywhere. Mom's only rule was to be home by suppertime. We kept the treasures we found in our clubhouse."

"Where is she?"

"She's gone."

"Did they move?"

"Her parents still live over on Oak Street." Clisty sank back on the thick, sofa pillows. "She's ... gone."

"She died?"

Clisty tried to shut out the terrible pictures in her mind. Suddenly, her eyes widened. She glanced at the mantle clock. "It's seven-thirty. There's time." She waved the clover back and forth in anxious hands. "I have to see Jake."

"Jake? Jake ... your cop ... Jake?"

"No ... yes. No, he's not *my* cop." She jumped up. "I found this four-leaf clover while we played. We took it home and sealed it between the contact-paper. I wrote the date on it with Magic Marker and gave it to Faith. She put it in her pocket. I told you. We were nine years old." Clisty paced. "We started to play Monopoly then sat on the floor and watched TV." When her eyes filled with tears, she pulled a hankie from her pocket.

"No," Becca grabbed a tissue. "You're still in camera-makeup. Now, slow down, breathe, and tell me what happened."

She blotted her tears with the tissue. "Mom had gone to the grocery. We started watching TV before we put our game away." She sniffed and tried to clear her throat.

"Then what?"

"Someone ... a big man in a sweaty shirt ... I can still smell him ... stormed into our house." She cringed as terrible mental images invaded.

"The man had a heavy beard and yellow teeth," she shuddered. "He grabbed us both by the wrist and dragged us toward the door." Clisty's voice drifted to a whisper while a horror-film played in her head. "I broke free, grasped Faith's hand and tried to pull her back; but, he was too big. I slipped on the Monopoly board and slid on a few cards and game pieces. I fell but scrambled to my feet, ran into the bathroom and locked the door. I heard the man snort something like, 'I got what I came for,' and stormed out the door with Faith."

"Oh, Clisty, how horrible! Where did they find her?"

"They didn't," she whispered. "She just vanished. It's been eighteen years. Her family has never given up," Clisty choked with tears. "I tried to save her." With a raspy voice she added, "With my angel on her kitchen windowsill, Grandma prayed for me every day."

She closed her eyes and slipped back into dark, frightening memories. "I know the prayers helped."

"Clisty, you were a child."

"I know. But, Becca, that witness in the surveillance video ... those eyes ... that was Faith. I'm positive of it." She looked at the clover in her hand and shouted, "This four-leaf clover proves she's alive! She sent it to me so I would look for her. Becca, I know where she is!"

I

News at Eleven - 2

"Let's go." Clisty placed her coffee cup on the table and grabbed the envelope with the precious four-leaf clover inside. "Hurry, Becca. The news will be back on at eleven."

"I know. I'm the producer." Becca fumbled with her yogurt container. Her spoon teetered on the saucer. "No, don't fall on the white area rug," Becca moaned.

"Don't worry about it." Clisty brushed it off, crossed the room and pulled her coat from the hall tree.

"Don't worry about it?" Becca questioned. "This, from the girl with a sterile home, except for the picture of two rag-a-muffins?"

"Okay, okay," Clisty agreed. She fished in her pocket for her gloves and car keys.

"Where are we going?" Becca asked. Outside, she slipped on the fresh powder of spring snow as she hurried behind. "The time is flying. You have to be behind the news desk before eleven."

"I know, Becca. But, I also know that was Faith in that ATM surveillance video. She's the bank robbery witness everyone is looking for and she's been missing for years." She fumbled with the remote entry button. The buzzer squawked and the two women jumped into the SUV.

The leather seats had grown cold. She shivered as she tried to force the key into the ignition.

Becca interrupted. "Wait a minute. I need to know where we're going." She patted Clisty's hand. "Take a deep breath and tell me what's going on."

Clisty let the motor idle. Her hand trembled on the floor shift. "Becca, the image in the ATM video was my friend, Faith."

"Honey, she was nine years old when she was kidnapped. That was eighteen years ago."

"I know," Clisty pounded on the shift knob. "But, I know Faith Sterling's eyes. That was her." Tears welled up and spilled down her cheeks.

"Don't mess up your makeup. You may not have time for a touch up before the late-night news." She patted Clisty's hand again. "Now, where are we going?"

"First, we'll stop at police headquarters and hope Jake is there." She looked right and left. It was early in the evening. On-coming lights sparkled on the windshield's frost patches. "I think I know where Faith is, but I don't know if it's safe to go there alone."

"Okay. With Jake along, I'll feel better." Becca buckled her seat belt. "Why didn't you just call or text him?"

"I'm a little scattered." Clisty pulled her phone from her pocket and pushed a button.

"Speed dial?" Rebecca teased.

"Never mind ..." Clisty put the receiver to her ear. "It's ringing ... pick up Jake." She disconnected and looked out at the road ahead. "He's on duty. Why doesn't he answer?"

"Leave a text message and let's go," Becca said urgently.

• • • • •

Clisty pulled into the police parking lot and had her hand on her seat belt clasp before the engine stopped. She flung the door open and dashed toward the door when Becca slipped a little as she stepped from the car.

"Becca, are you okay?" Clisty turned back quickly.

"Just trying to catch up. I'm wearing the wrong shoes for a hot pursuit."

Clisty waited at the door for her. "I'm sorry. You didn't hurt yourself, did you?"

"I'm fine," Becca assured her.

Outside, the daylight had slipped into early spring-evening darkness. But, inside the station, lights beamed in every corner. The smell of freshly popped corn penetrated the room. An officer jumped to his feet when Clisty walked in.

"Clisty Sinclair ... pardon me, Miss Sinclair," Jeremy Rhodes blustered. "What may I do for you?" He blushed as a few corn kernels fell from his uniform to the floor.

"That's alright. Call me Clisty." She paused and glanced around. "Is Detective Davis here?"

"No, Ma'am. Jake's been out since the bank robbery." He paused. "But, you know about the robbery. You broke the news at six."

"Yes ...," she frantically checked the room. "He hasn't come back?"

"No, Ma'am. He's interviewing the bank teller at the hospital. She was shot-up pretty bad."

"The hospital?" She turned to Rebecca. "He probably has his phone off if he's in the E.R. We'd better hurry on."

"Clisty, I don't know."

"I do," she snapped. Her texting thumbs flew over the phone's keypad. "Now, where are my keys?" she asked as she fumbled in her pocket. "I just had them."

A woman in a frayed coat scooped keys off the floor and handed them to the officer. He thanked her and turned the keys over in his hand. "Initial—P? And ... they're yours, Miss Sinclair?"

"Yes," Clisty allow a smile to lighten her face. "Grandma called me Pooky."

"Pooky?" He raised his eyebrows. "Where did your grand-parents live?

"Over on Norman Avenue."

"Six-twenty-four Norman Avenue, right?" Rhodes smiled.

"How did you know?"

"My parents bought their house when your grandparents moved to Florida. We lived there for seven years. When Mom and Dad had more kids, we moved. There was a little angel in the kitchen window. On the bottom was a name. Mom told me it was a Christmas Prayer Angel and we should pray for the person. Each person in the prayer partner exchange wrote their name on the bottom. It was Pooky."

Clisty gasped. "Grandma said she lost my angel, but she prayed for me every day anyway."

"Pooky," Rhodes whispered, "I've prayed for you since I was a kid." He paused then asked, "What happened about ten years ago, in the spring?"

"My boyfriend and I were in a car accident after the Senior Prom." She rubbed her finger over the initial on the key chain. "I was in a coma for two weeks."

"I could feel it," Rhodes whispered again. "Something seemed wrong. I prayed twice a day during that time."

Clisty took the officer's hand. "Thank you." Tears again threatened to drown her resolve. She looked away. "Becca, we'd better hurry." She gathered her keys and spoke again to Rhodes. "If Jake comes back and hasn't gotten my message, tell him I was here and to meet us at the clubhouse." She hurried out the door with Becca matching her steps.

"Maybe we should wait for Jake until he can be reached. He'll turn his phone on soon," Becca warned.

"We'll be fine," Clisty brushed off her concern and pulled her coat more tightly around her. The spring air had taken on a bitter chill.

• • • • •

Clisty reached for the car radio. "There may be more news about the robbery. Maybe they've found Faith."

"We just came from the Police Station. There was no news about the witness or the robber." Becca lowered her voice to a soothing whisper. "Clisty, Faith was kidnapped. If she's alive, where has she been and how did she get away?"

"I don't know. But, I'm going to where she directed."

"Directed?"

"Yes, the four-leaf clover. We kept the treasures we found at the clubhouse. I'm sure she'll try to meet me there."

"Where is it?" Becca asked.

"In my parents' back yard," Clisty said as she turned the corner and headed to the north side of town.

"I thought your parents were visiting your grandparents in Florida." Becca spoke slowly. "No one will be there."

"But, that has nothing to do with the clubhouse." Clisty downplayed the caution she heard in her friend's voice. "I can always get in there."

"I'm not thinking about ease of entry. I'm wondering how safe it will be to poke around in a dark backyard and shed."

"We'll be fine. It's my parents' yard." Clisty eased onto Keystone Avenue and followed the winding road into the next block. The street light in front of her parents' home was out.

"It looks dark," Becca gasped.

"Come on fraidy-cat." She popped the door open, jumped out and hurried toward the back of the house. A dog's bark in the distance hung on the crystal air. The cold gravel crunched under their feet.

"Clisty ... wait," Becca called in a hoarse whisper. As she tried to catch up, a dark figure approached them from behind.

Clisty strained to see into the darkness behind her. Dim light filtered through bony trees a few houses down. She saw something piled on the ground and gasped. She had just walked from that direction and there had been nothing there. "Becca?" she called into the darkness. There was no answer.

Fear gripped her chest as she crept closer. "Becca?" she whispered. Her eyes darted frantically from bush to each dense hedge around her.

"Oh ...," Becca moaned as she rolled over on her elbow. "What happened?"

Crack! A noise shattered the blackness around them. A large, burly figure about ten feet away staggered and fled from the yard. The shape of a woman wielding a large branch darted off in the opposite direction.

"Faith?" Clisty shouted frantically after her. The bells of the church on the corner chimed. It was eight p.m. News was at eleven.

I

News at Eleven - 3

"Jake!" Clisty called in relief as Detective Davis jumped out of his car in front of her parents' house. "You remembered the story about my childhood clubhouse!"

"Of course I did." He gathered her in his arms. "Clisty, who was that?" He pointed back to the person who had darted past him.

"Did you see her?" She gasped breathlessly.

"Her?" he questioned. "I saw him, the guy who beat it out of here as I pulled up."

"Then, you didn't see Faith?"

"No, I was watching the man."

"I wish I could have watched him!" Rebecca growled as she rubbed her shoulder. "He hit me."

"Are you okay?" Clisty asked and gently touched her. "Jake, you know Becca, my news producer."

"Right," he said. "You need to have that shoulder looked at." Then he asked, "Aren't you two supposed to be at the station right now? The news is on again at eleven."

"It's a long story." Clisty said as she put her arm around Becca. "Are you okay? Can you walk down to the corner coffee shop so we can fill him in?"

Becca flexed her arm. "I'm more angry than hurt." She raised her arm over her shoulder. "You fill him in. I'm still trying to catch up to what's happening."

"How is the bank teller?" Clisty asked. The snow started falling again and tiny ice flakes stung Clisty's nose and cheeks.

"She's conscious. Doctors say she'll mend," Jake said.

"You had better put your hood up, or your hair will have to be done again before the late news," Becca cautioned.

"If I put my hood up, I'll need a major overhaul, not a touch up." Clisty slipped a little and looked down. She had forgotten she was still wearing on-camera heals. Her feet were cold and had started to hurt. "These shoes weren't made for chasing criminals or ghosts."

"Ghosts? Here, you can hold on to me," Jake offered as he held out his arm. "What is going on?"

"Wow, arm and arm. Now, that's sweet," Becca cooed.

"Here, Becca, grab hold of my other arm," Jake offered.

• • • • •

Clisty stepped into the small, warm coffee emporium and rubbed her gloved hands together. "It feels good in here, Sharon," she said, smiling at the waitress. The wall-mounted TV whispered dialog, but she was too cold to pay attention. She scanned the menu above the serving counter. "My favorite is café mocha. I'd like an extra half shot of café and a double shot of mocha."

"Wow, with all that, it's my hips that would be shot," Becca moaned. "Coffee, black and a double shot of hot."

"Let's sit here by the window," Clisty suggested as she walked a few feet to a small table with four chairs clustered around it. "It's homey here."

"Hey, I thought I told you to get along home," Sharon snapped at a scruffy girl who slipped in behind Clisty and her friends.

"I'm cold," the child whispered.

"Then, sit right there," Sharon pointed to a bar stool in front of her. "Where's your mom?"

"She'll be here soon."

Clisty watched the frightened girl and smiled, but gave her the space she needed to warm up to her and the other strangers inside the Emporium.

At the table, Becca gulped as she leaned into the cold glass of the window. "Is that the guy in the hoodie again?"

The child gasped in fear and pulled her wet shoes up onto the seat and hugged her knees. She looked like a small turtle with every vulnerable part hidden.

"That's my husband on his way home from work," Sharon laughed and waved a full cup of coffee in his direction.

Clisty watched the child pull a tight, shabby coat around her. Sharon brought the steamy cups to the table and Clisty's focus shifted.

"I wondered about that guy too." Jake agreed.

"I'll hug the cup for warmth." She put her gloves in her pocket and blew across the surface of the coffee. "I'm warming my face with the rising, deliciously sweet steam." She closed her eyes and let the rising vapor warm her cheeks.

"I'd be happy to keep you warm," Jake offered.

Clisty looked at Becca to see if she had heard him. Becca raised her eyebrows. Over at the counter, big round, hollow eyes watched her sip the warm brew.

"Do you like cocoa?" Clisty asked the child.

"I think I had it one time." Her voice was as thin as she was, and as distant.

"Did you like it?" Clisty asked. The girl smiled. "Sharon, get her a big cup of your best hot chocolate." She smiled at her. "Will that be okay with your mama?" The child nodded a firm yes.

"When will your mother get back?" Jake asked. He lowered his voice. "I can't let a seven or eight-year-old run around town at night all alone."

"Probably when my cocoa's done," the girl said as she took tiny sips. "She'll meet me here."

Sharon wiped a cocoa ring from the counter. "Did that guy find you, Clisty?"

She froze inside and looked up slowly from her chocolate laced coffee. "Who? What guy?"

"He was tall and tattered, in a dark sweatshirt. I didn't tell him anything about you, Clisty. We've been friends since kindergarten. I've got your back." She slowed as she dried a cup and several spoons. "I wondered how he could be warm in ..."

Clisty's eyes grew large as she turned toward the darkness beyond the window. "When was he in here?"

"Was the sweatshirt a hoody?" Jake asked.

"Yes, he had it over his head but I could see his eyes. It was strange. He had the most beautiful brown eyes, sunk down in a face that belonged on an FBI most wanted poster." Sharon shuddered. "He scared me." She too looked out into the night. "He was in here just a little bit ago. I was glad when he left."

"Which way did he go?" Jake asked.

"Down toward your parents' place," Sharon nodded in Clisty's direction.

Clisty stiffened and Jake took her hand. She could feel his warmth caress her skin. She squeezed his palm and tried to relax. "Sharon, have you seen a young woman around here that isn't from the neighborhood?"

"Yes, that was another strange thing. Before you got here, this woman slithered around the side of the door and slipped in. It seemed to me she might have been dodging someone. Her eyes darted around the restaurant and she shifted back and forth."

Clisty's heart pounded as she held her breath. "And ...?"

"She said she saw you come in here earlier today and asked me to give this to you." Sharon reached into her apron pocket and drew out a pink plastic hair bow. "She said it's yours."

Clisty took the barrette from Sharon's hand and rolled it over and over. Tears came to her eyes and threatened to spill down her cheeks. She blotted them with a napkin. "Yes, it's mine," she whispered. "Becca," her voice cracked, "I gave this to Faith the morning of our last day together. Her hair kept falling in her eyes."

"Who is Faith?" Jake asked.

"She's your missing witness to the escaped bank robber suspect," Clisty announced. "I recognized her in—"

"The ATM video!" Sharon squealed and pointed to the TV. "I saw her on your newscast and thought she looked familiar. She had the same scar above her left eyebrow. Clisty, I thought someone had killed her years ago."

"That's what everyone thought, except her parents ... and me. This proves even more, that she's alive."

The child at the counter hopped down and slowly approached the small table. "No, Ma'am. That clip is mine," she announced.

"Yours?" Becca asked.

"Miss Sinclair said it belongs to her, Honey," Jake chimed in.

But the girl shook her head in defiance while willful curls slipped to her eyebrows. "No, it's not. It's mine." She grabbed the hair bow, wiggled back up onto the bar stool and took another gulp of hot chocolate with the barrette clasped tightly in her hand.

Clisty got up, slowly walked over and gently touched her small shoulder. "I had one just like it." Her eyes glistened. "I gave it to my very best friend in all the world." She started to reach out for it but stopped when the child pulled back. "What's your name?"

"My name's Pooky." She held the hair clip in both hands and drew it close in a caress. "My mama gave me the hair bow a long time ago."

Clisty wrapped her arms around the girl. "My name is Pooky, too. I think I know your mother." She looked over at Jake and Becca and smiled. "We have to hurry but I think we can find her before the eleven o'clock news."

I
News at Eleven - 4

"Sinclair," Clisty spoke into her cell. "What?" she gasped. "Okay. We're on our way."

Jake touched his phone screen. "Okay. Call SWAT," he said and turned to Clisty. "Sorry Babe. Gotta run."

"Me too." She folded her napkin. "That was the station, Becca. A news crew will meet us at 606 North—"

"Gramercy," Jake finished.

"Yes, how did—?"

"What's happening?" Becca pulled on her coat.

Clisty looked at Pooky who sat at the serving counter. She nodded to Sharon. "Can Pooky stay here and wait for her mother?" She gave the child a hug.

"Did you say, Gramercy?" the eight-year-old asked.

"Yes, but—"

"We were at a man's house on Gramercy," she said with wide eyes. "Is Mama there?"

"What man?" Jake asked.

"The man who brought us here."

"What did he look like, Honey?" he asked.

"He was tall and had a rough face." She sipped her drink. "He had on a dark blue sweatshirt."

Clisty looked from Jake to Becca. Fear stabbed her as she remembered the suspect in the bank robbery. Although missing for eighteen years, Faith could be that woman. "I want you to stay here, Pooky. Have you had supper?"

The eight-year-old looked up, "Sure. My cocoa."

"What else?" Clisty asked.

"Nothing," she whispered.

"Okay, Sweetheart. Miss Sharon can give you something hot."

"How about some creamy macaroni and cheese from the lunch special?" Sharon asked.

"That would be great," Clisty said. "I'll pay you later." She started for the door. "Oh, and keep her away from the news channel." She raised her eyebrows in emphasis.

Pooky hopped down from the stool and took Clisty's hand. "Let me come with you. Mama's there. I know she is."

"You need to stay and help Miss Sharon. I'll bet she has some jobs for you."

"Sure," Sharon drew out slowly. "You could wipe off the tables and I'll turn on the cartoon channel."

"That would be great," Clisty said as she hurried out the door. Outside, they started back to her parents' home for their cars.

"We need to hurry," Jake urged.

"Wait for me," Becca called out from behind. "Where are we going? It'll be a remote broadcast. I'll need to prepare."

"There's a standoff between a gunman and police over on North Gramercy," Clisty explained. "There's a female hostage. As information comes in, they'll feed it to us on location."

They slipped on the late season ice as they grabbed their car door handles and hopped in. "Follow me," Jake called out his car window as he made a U-turn in the middle of the street. "I'll lead the way with full lights and siren. Stay close behind me."

"Be careful," Clisty cautioned.

"You too, Babe."

As Jake reached out and placed the flashing lights on the roof, Clisty pulled her car in behind his and revved the engine. They flew past Sutton Place, Riverside and two other cross-streets until they came to Gramercy, about a half mile from the Coffee Emporium.

She slammed her foot on the brake and stopped in the middle of the street at the barricade. Clisty jumped out and reached for the microphone. Flattened early crocuses, bitten by the late snow and trampled by the television crew, were under her feet. She trembled, fearing the same outcome, but tried to stay professional.

With the ear piece placed in her ear, she stepped in front of the lens. "We're here in the middle of the six-hundred block of North Gramercy. All residences in the area—stay inside. I repeat—stay inside. If you are traveling, take Randolph Highway rather than North Gramercy and avoid this area. We have just arrived on the scene. We've been told that an armed gunman is holding a woman hostage." She motioned to a man who stood at the edge of the cordoned area. "Sir, tell us your name and what you saw?"

The middle-aged man cleared his throat. "I ... ah," the man's voice was shaky. "The name's Phil. I saw a rumpled man in a dark blue hoody pull a young woman out of an old truck and force her to walk into that house there at 606. I know I saw a hand-gun."

Clisty repositioned the mic. "Do you know if the man has been living in the house for very long?"

"The house had been for rent. I saw him last week a couple of times," he answered, his gaze still fixed on the house.

Clisty could feel panic grip her. Her palms felt sweaty inside her gloves and her stomach rolled and fell. "Did you see a young girl?"

"Right ... now that you ask, I do remember seeing a child when they first showed up. Not after that. Come to think of it, hardly the woman either, until late this afternoon."

"So, you saw the woman when they first arrived and then today?"

"I stopped over there about 4 pm with a pie my misses had made to greet them to the neighborhood and the woman answered the door. I said, 'Hello Mrs. ...' I thought she might fill in the last name, but she shook her head. She said he had only given them a ride to Fort Wayne. She started to say more but the man came up behind her. He started screaming at her. She slipped me an envelope before he slammed the door closed. She pointed to your name and TV station written on the outside."

"You brought it?" Clisty asked.

She heard an interruption behind her. "There, that's it." She turned as Pooky fell into her arms and held on tightly. "My Mama's in there," the girl sobbed.

"I am so sorry," Sharon gasped breathlessly. "She got away from me."

Still on camera, Clisty clung to the girl, in spite of Becca's direction to release her. "I'm holding a child I believe to be the hostage's daughter." She looked directly into the light. "She is safe with me." Her thoughts raced but she tried to stay calm. She hoped that those inside had a TV on. "Now, I'm talking to the man in the house." She smiled at Pooky. "The woman means nothing to you. You just gave her a ride home. I'm sure Faith is very grateful for your kindness. You can let her go now."

Jake stepped in front of the camera. "If you're watching, the bank teller is alive. Don't make things worse for yourself. Release the woman and we can help you make things right."

Clisty tried not to think of the danger Faith was in. She willed herself to sound calm. "Please, let her go. All little girls need their mother." She looked anxiously at the house but there was no movement. Suddenly, a car slid to a stop near the barricade. Faith's parents jumped out.

Clisty's eyes filled with tears as the Sterlings approached their granddaughter for the first time. "Ralph and Roma Sterling," she whispered, "this is Pooky. I believe she's your granddaughter."

They wrapped their arms around the child and sobbed. Silence fell like a warm presence as police and television crew looked on. The new grandmother looked at the house and whispered, "Please. Give her back."

The front door opened slowly but no lights were on. Darkness was everywhere. "Hold your fire. She's coming out," Jake shouted with a calm and steady voice.

With shaking hands held high, Faith Sterling slowly emerged, with a dark figure close behind, his hand on her shoulder. "Don't shoot," she shouted. "He wants to surrender."

A police woman took a few steps forward and stopped. Clisty whispered into the microphone. "She seems to be attempting a safe transfer."

"Let the woman step away from you," Jake announced into a bullhorn. "Lay down on the ground with your hands behind your head."

The next events happened so fast, Clisty couldn't breathe. The man fell onto the cold, wet ground. Officers wrapped his wrists in handcuffs. Her dear friend, Faith, ran forward and embraced all those who had waited eighteen years for her to come home. She sobbed as she grabbed Pooky and fell into her parents' arms.

Clisty whispered a prayer of thanksgiving and praise as she wiped tears from her face. Rebecca and all those around were visibly unable to fight back their own emotions.

Faith reached out to Clisty and cried in her arms. "I knew you'd find me if I could get here."

Clisty looked into the camera but, no matter how hard she tried, words would not come. Finally, she whispered, "My friend Faith was kidnapped eighteen years ago. Finally ... praise God, she has come home." She hugged her and beamed. "This has been news of a true miracle in Fort Wayne ... to be seen at eleven."

Part II
Safe - 1

When the camera lights went out, the night seemed even darker to Clisty than it had been before the spotlight shone on the little house on North Gramercy. The stand-off between the suspected bank robber and the police was over. Firearms were quickly stored in the SWAT van and protective vests removed and stashed. Faith Sterling had walked out of the house on her own, finally free from a past she had endured for eighteen years. But, was it possible she had escaped her nightmares that easily?

Becca sighed deeply and blew the fresh air out slowly. "Wow! What a story," she said as she started to help Clint, the camera man load the equipment. "Not so sure I'm ready for another one of those, though. I think my heart stopped beating twenty minutes ago."

Clisty still held the WFT-TV microphone in her slender fingers when she grabbed Faith in her arms and sobbed. "You're home! Where have you been?" She pulled back at arm's length to look at her lost friend. Clisty gasped loudly, the shock was more than she could silence. She felt chilled from the penetrating night wind. What she saw when she searched Faith's face for the friend she use to know, frightened her.

Faith's beautiful eyes were lost in sunken, dark gray pools of fear and emptiness. With trembling hands, she tried to brush matted hair from her forehead, leaving streaks of smeared perspiration behind. She looked at Clisty with a flat, glassy stare and then stiffened as she stuffed her hands in the pockets of her long, faded cotton skirt. A rumpled, heavy knit sweater hung open around her wrinkled peasant blouse. Her clothes smelled like musty socks.

"Oh Faith," her mother cried as she approached her with open arms. "Thank God! Thank God!" Her words dissolved in the tears that streamed down her face. She too clung to the daughter she had not seen since she was nine years old. "How can it be? Only God could have brought you home."

Pooky stood behind the three women, outside the circle of love. She patted the small of her new grandma's back. "What's wrong with Mama?" she whispered as she tried to get close to her. But, her mother said nothing. Faith seemed frozen except for her hands. "Why are your hands shaking, Mama?"

Faith's glistening eyes darted to her daughter. Her tears seemed to refuse to stop flowing and she fixed her expression on some distant memory. "Shaking?" she asked, seemingly unaware of her surroundings, lost in the fear and trauma of hours of staring into the end of a revolver.

"She's a little overwhelmed right now, Honey," Roma explained as she turned and bent down to her granddaughter's level. She touched the soft cocoa smudged cheek of the grandchild she didn't know existed.

"Did Miss Sinclair say you're Mama's mama?" Pooky asked with a puzzled expression that began to grow stern. "Mama said to find you. Where have you been?"

"Yes, Sweetheart," her grandmother said as she finally started to shed eighteen-year-old tears. "I'm your grandma and," she clasped the tips of her husband's fingers, "and this is your grandpa. We have been right here, waiting for you. We didn't know where you were."

"Grandpa?" Pooky asked, quickly jerking back a step as her eyes grew large and fearful. A dog's distant bark caused her to startle.

"It's all right, Pooky," Clisty soothed. "I have known your mama's daddy all my life and he's a good man. He has waited a long time to be a grandpa. I'll bet he's rehearsed it over and over."

Pooky eyed the man who would be Grandpa. "Like, when I played Red Riding Hood at school?"

"Just like that," Clisty patted her head. "Where did you go to school?" Like any broadcast journalist, she began to collect the details she would need to pursue the full story of Faith's abduction. But, the news story was only part of it. She had to know where her friend had been. She had imagined every possible location in the years since she was gone. Except for a twist of fate that freed her from the grip of the man who captured Faith, she too would have vanished those long years ago.

Pooky folded her arms and closed herself off to the people around her. "I don't go to school any more. I only went there a couple of weeks. Daddy said I could go, but then Grandpa said, no." Her voice faded as she turned her chin up, defiantly, at Ralph. "I never got to be in the play after all."

"I'm sorry to hear that," Clisty said as she tried to think fast. "Can you remember the name of the school or anything you saw?"

"The name? No." She twisted back and forth and wrinkled up her nose.

Becca watched her and coached, "You're a good observer. When you're as old as I am, you'll need glasses to see what's around you. I've noticed you see everything. Did you see anything that would remind you of the school?"

"There was a sign out front with a big dog on it," the child's eyes shone with pride. "I remembered some. That was good, wasn't it?"

"Yes, it was. I wouldn't have noticed that, I'm sure," Becca encouraged her.

"That was very good." Clisty put her arm around Pooky's shoulder.

"You smell good," she blurted out as she nuzzled a little longer in Clisty's arm.

"Thank you. I'll share a little bit of my perfume with you and your mama in a few days." Things were going too fast for Clisty's tired mind. She wondered how a young girl could possible keep up. "Your mother is going to go to the hospital in the ambulance now. I'm going back to the studio for the last newscast of the day." She looked up at Faith's parents and smiled. "You can ride with your grandparents."

"No!" Pooky announced and pulled out of Clisty's embrace. "I want to go with Mama."

The first responder reached out and took Pooky's hand. "That's okay. You can ride in the ambulance with your mother. Your grandparents can follow us in their car. You'll see Grandma and Grandpa when we get to the hospital." He guided Faith onto the gurney.

"I'll stop by after the newscast and make sure everyone is all right," Clisty whispered as she leaned down to hug the young girl. "Okay?"

"Okay." Pooky's eyes darted from her mother to all the new faces around her.

"It's okay, Honey," Faith's words escaped from her mouth like they were riding on the last breaths she would take. She turned to her old friend and motioned for her to come closer.

Clisty leaned down toward her. "I love you, Faith," she said and rubbed the back of her hand against her cheek.

"I ... I ...," Faith stammered, as her chin quivered and her voice choked.

"I know, Honey," Clisty tried to help.

"I have to ... ah ... ah ...," she rattled in aimless monotone, "... tell you." She closed her eyes hard and slowly warned. "He's coming, you know. He's coming ...."

"Who, Faith ... who's coming?"

"I'm sorry, Clisty," the EMT worker urged. "She needs to be evaluated."

"Evaluated?" Faith mumbled. Her voice was thin and weak. "Like a test? I ... don't like tests."

"You rest," the attendant said as he patted her shoulder. "We gotta go," he warned Clisty again. Faith lay back on the gurney and seemed to disappear on the mat, like she had eighteen years ago, a ghost among the living.

"I know," Clisty watched with shock. "I can see." Bending near her friend's ear she whispered, "I'll go to the studio and finish the broadcast. This breaking news tape will roll again on the eleven o'clock news. Then, I'll stop by the hospital and check on you."

"That will be terribly late," Becca reminded her, then shrugged. "Maybe sleep is over-rated."

"I'll stop by," Clisty repeated. "It can't possibly be too late for me. I promise I won't awaken you."

• • • • •

Clisty slid into her chair behind the news desk at WFT and quickly clipped on her lapel microphone, racing the clock. It was ten-fifty-five. Her hands trembled. She took a deep breath and held it in her lungs for a few seconds. She didn't have stage-fright. She had been running on one-hundred percent adrenaline since the six o'clock news exposed the grainy ATM video of her friend. Faith had been lost so long ago she remained the pigtailed girl in summer cotton shorts and stripped t-shirt in Clisty's mind. When she closed her eyes, she could still hear the faint laughter of two nine-year-olds on a sunny afternoon adventure.

"Two minutes, team," Becca called from behind the camera.

The junior anchor exhaled slowly, blowing the air silently through her lips. She had to keep her wits about her. She had to tell the story without telling it all, to keep details about Faith's rescue for police use only, without the public's awareness of the lack of transparency.

Suddenly, the hot lights flooded Clisty's face and the newscast began. She looked down momentarily while the film from the remote broadcast ran again and was amazed to see she was still wearing what she had on at 6 pm. It had only been five hours, but a lifetime had caught up to her in those few hours. Her mussed skirt hid under the desk but the collar of her shirt that should have stayed beneath her suit jacket, refused to lay flat. She quickly tried to give it a finger-ironing.

Clisty began on cue. "The stand-off between the police and the person, who may have held up the bank, lasted for more than hour. The police have identified the man as Melvin Dean Fargo. As you saw from the footage that just re-aired from our on-the-scene breaking news report, the woman who came out of the house ahead of the suspect, probably saved Fargo's life," Clisty reported. "She warned the police that he was surrendering, which avoided a barrage of bullets if authorities believed the woman was still a captive."

Dan Drummond fidgeted in the chair beside her; his hand was itchy on his pen as he anxiously flipped it up and down. "Yes, Clisty, and—"

"... and, the police consider her a hero, Dan," she smiled into the camera.

Dan began, "She is the woman, who, eighteen years ago—"

"I'm glad you brought that up," Clisty deliberately interrupted. "Police are keeping the woman's identity from the public at this time."

Dan paused and shook his head slightly. "In case the suspect had accomplices?"

"That could be a reason for withholding her name," Clisty suggested, then quickly added as Drummond opened his mouth to say more. "I pledge to bring you the entire background surrounding this event in the days to come." Clisty was afraid, if permitted to speak Dan could have given too much information and would have hijacked the story from her capable hands.

Dan's jaw dropped. With a skillful recovery he added, "We will all be waiting to hear the details of these remarkable events."

"And, in other news," Clisty began again, "the Park Service has announced a new member of the lion pride at the Fort Wayne Zoo. A male cub named, Scruffy, was born at eight-twenty this evening, a fitting addition to our evening of new beginnings."

Dan stared into the camera with a forced smile and set jaw. "Thank you for watching. That's the News at Eleven."

• • • • •

"Well," Dan started cautiously as he jerked the mic from his shirt, "it sounds like you have scored quite a story for yourself." He pulled his tall lanky legs from under the desk and unbuttoned his suit coat from around his middle-aged belly.

"Dan," she began slowly to maneuver around the minefield of news-room protocol. Clisty knew that the senior-anchor has first chance at significant stories. A junior anchor simply does not grab stories from the top of the pile and run with them. "I am sorry," she started again, "but the backstory of this woman's life is my story as well."

"Your story? I thought that was up to—"

"No, I didn't mean it that way." She fumbled with words to express the unique situation she was in. The set cleared, Becca waited in the back of the studio. "Dan, you don't understand," Clisty tried to explain.

They left Studio-A silently and walked into the outer hall. Dan collected his hat and coat with a snap and an attitude. "I can easily see I don't." Then he turned, "How is it that this woman's story is magically yours?"

"Dan," Clisty looked around her cautiously, to see if other ears could hear. "The woman is Faith Sterling. She was my childhood friend-of-the-heart. A man kidnapped her right out of my grasp, in my own living room, when we were both nine-years old. Then ... she just vanished. While the police apprehended the suspected bank robber, they haven't tracked down and brought to justice the man who took Faith all those years ago. She is very confused and fragile right now, and may be in danger from her captor. The police want to keep the circle small of those who have contact with her. They hope she will remember me and trust me, since we were inseparable as children. So, I will be getting her story. I hope you understand."

"Clisty," Dan removed the hat he had just put on and crumpled it in his hand. "I understand now. Her backstory is indeed your story, too. If there is anything I can do to help, just let me know. I'll be praying for both of you."

"Thanks Dan. You're the second person who said that to me tonight." Her mind followed a tangential path back to the Christmas angel that sat on her spotless mantle. "I appreciate your prayers."

II
Safe - 2

Everything looked white and colorless when Clisty walked into Faith's hospital room. Life and color, nearly sterilized out of the entire building, lay barely breathing in front of her. It was true, Clisty did like simple, monochromatic décor in her own home, but in this room it was different. The crisp white cover on the hospital bed hardly moved. Clisty studied the body of the stranger, yet friend, who didn't appear to have enough energy to breathe. Stranger—yes—but oh how Faith looked like her mother now that she was an adult. Clisty's own blue eyes filled with tears.

"If you study her closely, you'll see she's still with us," a familiar voice spoke softly from the corner of the room.

"Jake!" Clisty gasped in a hoarse whisper and jumped. "You startled me." She didn't take her eyes off her friend. "Do you think she's asleep or in a comma?"

"I talked to the nurse when I got here. She said that Faith is lost inside herself right now, trying to heal by sleeping. The nurses come in every half hour, rouse her and direct her to breathe more deeply."

"Imagine, being so exhausted you forget to breathe," Clisty shook her head.

"Come and sit here beside me." He patted the empty chair beside him and then rested his hand on the back. "It's about eleven-thirty. You should be at home but I know you want to be here. They'll come back in a little while to talk to her."

Clisty removed her coat and placed it over the arm of the chair and, with one motion, sank onto the cushion. "What are you doing here?" But, she didn't look at him. She fixed her gaze on Faith.

"I watched your late newscast here in Faith's hospital room," he gestured toward the television that glowed from its mounted brackets on the wall. "I turned it down so it wouldn't bother Faith. But, I can still hear it."

When Clisty adjusted her senses to the lower volume, she could also hear Faith's shallow respiration. The room was quiet. Everything was still. Faith didn't move, but all eyes were on her. "Then you heard my pledge to follow the story into the past," she whispered.

"I did. That's why I'm here, too. If she tells you anything, it might help us apprehend her captor." He reached above the chair back and rubbed Clisty's shoulder.

His closeness felt warm and inviting, but she couldn't relax yet. "Then, we can work together on this?"

"Absolutely." He sipped from the coffee vendor cup he held and looked inside as he swished it around the rim. "Besides, I wanted to see how you're doing. It's been a long day for you. I knew you would come here before going home."

"I'm okay." She brushed off Jake's concern. While she liked his interest, she would not give in to her exhaustion. Then she turned and saw his skeptical expression and changed the subject. "Where did you get the coffee?"

"From the machine in the lounge; I'll get some for you, but it's not very good," he offered as he studied the cup in his hand. "How about some cocoa?"

"That would be even better," she agreed and then added, "I admit ... I am very tired but I really am fine."

As he started to stand up, he smiled and slowly removed his arm from around her. "I'll be right back."

"Thanks, Jake." She leaned her head back and closed her eyes.

"You'll be asleep by the time I get here with your hot chocolate," he said as he paused at the door.

"I hope not. I want to be awake when they rouse her again." Clisty didn't open her eyes but smiled as Jake closed the door.

It felt so good to finally relax, she fought her body's need to let go and sleep. Her muscles twitched as mental pictures of two happy girls danced in her head, riding their bikes to the park and skating on Miller's Pond in the winter. One day, she and Faith rode in her dad's truck with him as he drove out onto the thick ice to where his friend, Ed, had set up a small fishing shack. All four of them sat on small wooden stools around the hole in the ice through which he fished. The images warmed her like the camp stove that stood in the corner of the shack, where Ed made gooey marshmallow s'mores over the heat.

Ring! The room phone dissolved the precious images and rattled Clisty's rest. She may have nodded off a little she admitted to herself. She jumped up and paused first, to steady her sleepy legs before she moved, then darted across the room to answer it before Faith awakened. "Hello?" she said softly.

The caller said nothing at first. All Clisty could hear was the dead air of an open line and ... just perhaps, some breathing on the other end. "Hello?" she said again.

"Let me talk to Jocelyn," a rough male voice demanded.

"Jocelyn? You must have the wrong room," she started to replace the receiver when she heard a female voice on the line.

"Please, Ma'am, put ... Faith on the phone," the person asked with a tremor in her voice.

"Who is this?" Clisty nearly dropped the receiver as her heart pounded.

"Never mind that," a scuffle was heard on the line. "Gimme that phone," the man shouted at the woman.

Just then Jake came back into the room carrying a cup of hot chocolate. Clisty motioned for him to come to her side. She had to be strong, to keep her wits about her, so she held the receiver away from her ear, allowing Jake to listen in. Jake put the cocoa on the bed table and waited. Clisty pointed to the receiver and grabbed his shirt in her fist to draw him closer.

"You listen to me, girly," the gruff man barked. "You put Jocelyn on this phone right now."

"I'm sorry, there is no Jocelyn here." She thought quickly and asked, "Where are you calling from?" Hoping to get some information, she waited frantically for the answer.

"That ain't got nothin' to do with nothin', Missy," he growled. "You don't need to know where I am. You just need to put Jocelyn on this phone, now!"

"Well, if you're calling long distance ..." she thought fast, "I wouldn't want to keep you on the line very long and run up your phone bill." She looked at Jake for assurance.

"Please," the woman begged again.

"There is no Jocelyn here," Clisty repeated. When she saw Faith stir a little, she hurried the conversation. "Sorry. Have a good evening." With the receiver replaced on the phone cradle, she buried her head in Jake's chest. "He asked for Jocelyn, Jake. But, the woman asked for Faith. She knew her real name."

"Try to remember all they said, Clisty," Jake coached her. "I'll write it all down." He pulled a small notebook from his inside jacket pocket.

"They really didn't say anything," she tried to clear her tired head so she could think. "The man asked to speak to Jocelyn and when that didn't work, the woman asked for Faith. That was him! I'm sure of it. I will never forget his meanness." Her eyes darted from Jake to the hospital bed. "They've found her," she gasped.

"But, it didn't sound like they were here, not in Fort Wayne," Jake assured her. "Since he took her so many years ago, he may suspect that she would have tried to come home." He put his arms around her and rocked her back and forth. "Was there anything else?"

"No information really but ... flavor, a sickening taste in my mouth, bitter, awful." She pulled back and stared out the window into the night. "He was gruff in manner, demanding, cold. He used poor English, 'ain't' and 'girly.'" She rubbed her forehead and tried to force herself to think. "The lady was gentler. She caved in to the man's demands. She sounded a little more educated, maybe ... oh, I don't know. They were on the line for such a short time."

"You did great, Honey. You learned a lot in a matter of a few sentences." Jake gathered her in his arms again and pulled her close.

"No," Faith gasped with a frail voice. With closed eyes, she kicked and flailed her arms like she was fighting someone off.

"Faith, Honey," Clisty soothed her by trying to stroke her forehead.

"No," Faith fought her off and slapped her hand away.

"Faith, it's me, Pooky," she tried again but was careful not to touch her this time.

"Pooky? Where is she? Where's Pooky?" She rose up slightly on her elbow and looked around the room with eyes that didn't seem to see.

"It is a very long story, Faith. But, your daughter, Pooky is safe. She's with your parents." How much she wanted to hold her friend but did not make another attempt for fear of frightening her.

"Mama and Daddy?" she asked with a strained expression, her eyes large with fear. "No, no!" She looked around the room, searching every corner.

"You're in the hospital in Fort Wayne, Indiana, Honey," Clisty assured her.

The lost child-woman nodded, like the words sounded familiar but her surroundings were foreign to her. "Where?" She nodded again. "Where am I? Where is Pooky?"

"Faith—"

"Who is Faith?" she questioned as she drew her fists up to her temples and massaged them frantically. "I don't know Faith anymore. I don't know what you're saying," she cried.

A nurse in a blue uniform came crisply into the room. "Oh good, you're awake. I'm Kim and I'm your nurse tonight."

"But, she's so—" Clisty whispered through her tears.

"I know ... confused. She's been through a lot." Kim came over to the bedside and reached for Faith's wrist but she immediately jerked away. "I'm sorry," she spoke gently. "I was just so happy to see your big beautiful eyes, I moved too quickly." Kim patted Faith's arm.

"Try ... calling her Jocelyn," Jake offered.

Faith's expression softened a little. "Jocelyn," she agreed.

"All right then." Kim placed her hand slowly on Faith's forearm. "I would like to pick up your hand, Jocelyn, and take your pulse. Is that okay with you?"

Faith said nothing at first. "Pulse? I ... I don't understand."

"I'll hold your hand just above the palm," Kim began slowly, "then touch your wrist gently. Okay?"

Faith nodded as she laid her head back in an attempt to catch her breath. Suddenly, she threw her hand to her chest as a look of panic crossed her face.

"Nurse ...?" Clisty covered her mouth with her hand as she tried to gain composure. Frightened by what she saw, she feared for Faith's ability to come back to her mentally.

"She's hyperventilating," Kim explained. "She has been breathing very shallow since she came in and now she's panicking."

To Faith she explained, "I'm going to put my hand on your diaphragm. I want you to breath by pushing on my hand." Slowly, Faith began to calm and breathe normally. "Good. Now, see there. Your respirations are much better."

With her patient stabilized, Kim spoke to Clisty and Jake in hushed tones on the other side of the room. "Except for the episode just now, she is doing as good as can be expected. Before she can remember who she is, she has to have more energy. Her crushed spirit is very fragile. Our first goal is—we want her to be able to inhale and exhale."

Then she turned to her patient. "Jocelyn, I'm going to put an oxygen cannula on your nose. You don't need to be frightened. It will help you breathe."

Faith watched the cannula come close to her face and nodded. "Lady, too," she said as she began to breathe more naturally. She looked up at Clisty and gasped in a moment of recognition. "Pooky?" she asked.

"Yes," Clisty nodded as tears streamed down her cheeks. She reached in her pocket and pulled out the clover sealed in frayed, wrinkled plastic. Folding it into Faith's hand, she closed her fingers around it.

Faith glanced down at the small scrap of her childhood she had shielded for eighteen years then looked at her friend with tired eyes. Taking Clisty's hand, a flash of fear crossed her face and she pulled her close. "Pooky ..." she begged, "keep Little Pooky safe. He'll be coming for us. He always said he would." She closed her eyes while tears ran down her face. "He's coming again you know."

II

Safe - 3

The next morning, Clisty returned and settled into the chair in the corner of Faith's hospital room. "I'm glad it's Saturday. I won't have to be at the studio this afternoon" The aroma of freshly baked sugar cookies filled the room. Roma had artfully arranged them on a small platter and placed them on the over-the-bed table.

"Your parents will be home from Florida this afternoon, won't they, Clisty?" Roma asked as she fluffed Faith's bed pillow.

"Yes, and I'm glad." Then she smiled sheepishly. "I'm an adult with serious adult responsibilities, but with everything that happened yesterday, it feels good that they will be home."

"When life becomes complicated, it's nice for us to pull our family and friends closer around us, isn't it?"

Clisty smiled the smile of sweet memories. Outside, the April day was magnificent. There was no evidence of snow remaining in black, left-over piles along curbs. Pale green tree leaves had pushed out and demanded consistent spring temperatures.

"Yes, it's always nice to have family around," Clisty said, "but especially when the world seems to have tipped a little and things are listing to starboard. I'm glad it's such a beautiful day. Everything about it is glorious, from the blue sky to the fact that Faith is home."

Roma started to respond, and then her eyes grew large in pleasant anticipation. "Well, Pooky, I wondered when you would wake up." She walked over to the bed, reached out and gave her granddaughter a long hug. "It's nice that the hospital allowed you to curl up and nap with your mama this morning." She smiled as she watched her new granddaughter yawn and stretch. When Pooky spied the platter of cookies, Roma added, "I don't usually serve children cookies for breakfast, but this is a special occasion."

"Hi, Miss Sinclair," Pooky collected the biggest cookie on the plate, bounced down off the bed, went over and planted her feet in front of Clisty. She was so close, the toes of her shoes touched Clisty's brown, lace up Saturday shoes. "Grandma said you're a friend of Mama's." She bit into the sweet smelling, iced cookie as crumbs fell into Clisty's lap.

"That's right. I hadn't seen her in a long time and I really missed her." She brushed the cookie specks from her jeans and smiled.

Pooky pressed herself against the side of Clisty's leg and silently slipped up onto her lap. "Mama talks funny, but I can understand her, a little. She said I could trust you." The girl snuggled back on Clisty's arm and rested her head on her shoulder.

"Disinhibited Reactive Detachment Disorder," Roma whispered without looking at Pooky. "This whole thing must have set her back. She seems to let anyone get close to her, except Al."

"Maybe she always did. Who knows what her life was like?" Clisty suggested.

"Who, Grandma?"

"Someone Miss Sinclair and I know, Honey." Roma brushed off the question as she perked up and listened. "It sounds like your mama may be finished with her shower. I heard the water turn off."

"She's taking a shower?" Pooky asked as she picked up the locket Clisty wore around her neck.

"Yep. Do you want to shower when she's finished? I'm sure it will be okay with the nurse. She's kinda kept her eye on you too this morning."

"Maybe." Pooky turned the locket over to see the engraved flowers on the back. "I want to stay with Mama."

"Do you want to see the picture?" Clisty watched Pooky's eyes and curious fingers inspect the necklace.

Pooky nodded and tried to force her chewed fingernails down into the place where the front clasped to the back. "I ain't got no fingernails." She hung her head in resignation, her bottom lip protruded like a perch outside a bird house.

"So I see," Clisty tried to ignore the pads at the ends of Pooky's fingers that stood proud of her nails, gnarled down to nothing. Clisty looked up at Roma. "Maybe Grandma has some pretty pink fingernail polish. Would you like that?" Pooky nodded vigorously. "You might have to stop biting your nails if you want to keep them pretty."

"Can we Grandma?" Pooky jump down, ran to her grandmother and grabbed her hand.

"Can you what?" Faith shuffled a little as she came into the room in a clean shirt and jeans. She had gained enough energy to wrap her arms around her daughter as she eased onto the side of the bed. "What are you planning to do?"

"We were talking about painting Pooky's fingernails a pretty, Petal Pink. Is that okay?" Roma asked as she placed a cup of coffee on the bedtable. She had brought it in a thermos from her own coffee pot at home. "I assume you drink coffee. I can find some tea if you prefer."

"No, coffee is wonderful. Steven and I drank coffee each morning."

"Steven?" Clisty asked as Roma handed her a cup from the basket she had brought in.

"Who?" Faith asked as Pooky hopped over and tried to help her mama lean back on the elevated hospital bed.

"Steven. You said you and Steven drank coffee each morning. Was that before he went to work?"

"Work?"

"Steven, where did he work, Faith?" Clisty tried again.

"He …," Pooky began.

"No, Pooky," Faith whispered in frightening gasps. "Nothing." She sipped silently from her cup and glimpsed out the window with darting eyes.

"Can you tell us about the man who brought you to Fort Wayne?" Clisty asked.

"I don't remember," Faith stated flatly. Suddenly, the coffee began to slosh a little in the cup she held in trembling hands.

"I was asleep," Pooky said, as Faith pulled her onto the bed beside her.

"Let's rest a little, Honey," Faith gently patted her daughter's forehead. She leaned back on the bed and closed her eyes.

"I'd better leave and let you sleep." Clisty started to place her cup on the windowsill. "I can come back after you have napped."

"No, please," Faith reached out her hand. "I ... I think I know you." Her eyes, rimmed in red, shed fresh tears that flowed down her cheeks. "I'm sorry." From her pocket she pulled a tissue and blotted the corners of her eyes. The plastic covered clover fell out with it. She picked up the "lucky piece" and then looked at Clisty. "No, no ... I do know you, Clisty. But ... I was told that you were killed the day I was taken." With her hand held flat on her chest, she began patting herself as a mother would calm a child. "I ... don't know what's true anymore."

With eyes still closed, Pooky reached up and stroked her mother's cheek. "It's okay, Mama."

Faith patted her daughter's hand. "I know only what they told me. I lived in one room."

"Not all the time, I'll bet," Clisty cautiously coaxed. "You said Pooky went to school for a few weeks."

"But, I never went out of the house," Faith sighed. "Just Pooky."

"That was when Grandpa was gone," Pooky's eyes snapped open. "I don't know where he was."

"Jail ... I think," her mother said softly, with little expression or concern, as if she were talking about a stranger.

"Did Mama teach you to read and write and work numbers?" Roma asked. "You know I was a teacher for a long time."

"Yes," Pooky's eyes flew open in amazement. "How did you know?"

"Because I taught her when she was little."

Clisty's heart jumped as she thought of a question that demanded an answer, but she didn't know how to ask it. "You know I have to ask you, Faith," she began with a smile and compassionate tone. "Where did you go to school?"

"School?" her eyes blinked and stared into apparent nothingness. "I don't remember," she stammered.

Clisty's heart hurt for her friend and she choked on the next question. "You don't remember school?"

"I don't remember leaving the house, ever," Faith sighed deeply. "I saw children from my upstairs window. They played in some yards down the block, but I could see them down there. I could hear them, too. I saw some of them play tennis in the street once. Our house was on a road that made a circle a few streets down."

"A cul-de-sac?" she asked.

"I don't know what that is," Faith's voice drifted off. "He caught me standing near the window one time and beat me."

"Who did, Faith? Was it that man who kidnapped you?" Clisty thought of the smelly man with rotting teeth.

"Kidnapped? What do you mean ... kidnapped?"

Clisty searched for words that clearly were not in Faith's vocabulary, to explain what had happened. "Do you remember, a long time ago, when we were watching television at my house? A man burst in the door and tried to take both of us, to steal us. I got away."

Great moans of grief heaved up from deep inside Faith as her face twisted and distorted. "Why didn't you come with me, Pooky?" A flood of tears angrily raced down her cheeks. "Why did you abandon me?"

"What?" Clisty gasped.

"You ran away and let him take me," Faith sobbed.

"We were nine years old, Faith," Clisty cried.

"Honey," Roma quickly interrupted, "a child can't fight off a full grown man."

"I know ... I know," Faith sobbed. "But ... I was so lonely," she whispered as she closed her eyes. "He told me that Momma and Daddy sold me to them."

"Oh, Sweetheart, you didn't believe them did you?" her mother threw her hand to her mouth in shock.

"No ... they told me every day ... but I didn't believe it one time." A faint smile crossed her lips. "I won every day that I didn't believe their lies."

Clisty cleared her throat and tried to not sound hurt by what her friend had said. "Then, I bet it became hard to know how to tell the lies from the truth."

"It was hard, I guess," Faith swallowed and cleared her throat. "Clisty, I never really blamed you. I just couldn't stand not having any friends. I did my studies in my room, read, everything in the one space. I could come to the table in the kitchen for dinner sometimes.

My mother," she stopped and looked up at Roma, "my other mother came to my room to teach me. Once in a while, we'd play games."

"It sounds like she cared for you," Roma offered softly.

"I guess."

Clisty knew she had to gather more information if they were ever going to find those who took her friend. "What was her name?"

"Name?" Again, Faith stared with a blank expression. "I ... don't know."

Clisty tried another approach. "Did you have a TV or radio in your room?" The questions continued but Faith's response was always an empty gaze.

"Television," Faith remembered with a smile. "I could watch Mr. Rogers when I was little. It was an old TV set. I couldn't watch very often. They would come in and take a tube out of the back when they didn't want me to watch anymore."

Clisty fished for words when all the ones she had used were all the ones she could think of. "What did you do the rest of the time?"

"I slept a lot ... I guess. I don't know," she closed her eyes again. "Oh," she opened her eyes and, for a moment, they sparkled. "I wrote letters to you, almost every day, for about a year. I couldn't mail them, so I found a hole in the wall of my closet and put them in there. I pretended it was my mailbox." With Pooky in her arms, she snuggled and kissed the top of her head.

"I wish I had gotten them," Clisty whispered.

"You did ... in my dreams," Faith said as her voice danced in the space between awake and asleep. "We would play and laugh and ..." she drifted off and her breathing seemed to become normal again.

"You were in my dreams too," Clisty added. But, what she didn't say was, her dreams were actually nightmares.

II
Safe - 4

"I am so glad you and Daddy are home," Clisty exhaled in relief later that day. There, in her parents' living room, with the comfortable deep, down-filled pillows of the couch supporting her, she was at home and felt safe. Her apartment, stripped clean of color and memories, except for the Prayer Angel that sat on her spotless mantel, was far different from her parents' home. Nearly every inch of the tables and bookshelves held memories displayed in pictures, a multitude of books, her mother's pottery collection, and the little clay self-statue Johnny Swanson had given his favorite elementary school teacher.

"Usually, I just pick up my phone and call you," Clisty admitted, "but ... now I see how fragile life can be. I want you close by; then I know, God is in his heaven and all's right with the world."

"Well, I know God can make all things right, Honey. But, speaking of your phone, you do use it a lot. I'm more concerned about that thing. I bet you sleep with it." Concern for her daughter was just part of who Carol was. Her smile was so much like Clisty's anyone could easily see that the daughter was part of the mother as well.

"I don't sleep with it," she protested reluctantly. "Actually, it's on the bedside table."

"See, I told you." Carol Sinclair threw both hands up in victory. "I read an article about how all this technology is actually making people feel less attached, rather than more."

"Mother, I'm not playing games on the thing. Rebecca, or the station manager, has to be able to reach me when there's breaking news." She felt her cell vibrate in her phone pouch, pulled it out and checked the message.

"Putting that thing in a pretty Bradley cell phone cross-body does make it easier to keep it close-by, but it makes it harder to get away from, too."

"Mom, I can't get away from it." She shook her head as if to correct what she had said. "I don't want to get away from it." Clisty didn't want to argue, and the truth was they rarely did. Still, she often had a sense that her mother didn't think her job was "real work" because she did it in front of a camera. "The station depends on me to deliver the news, not just about the birth of baby lion cubs, but about a standoff between police and a bank robber, with a dear friend caught in the middle."

"You certainly experienced all of that, didn't you?" her mother agreed. "Clisty," her voice grew soft, "I don't say it often enough, but I am so proud of you. The part you played in Faith's story yesterday was amazing." Then she added, "And the cute little lion cub named Scruffy was great too."

Clisty laughed. "You were watching in your hotel room, Friday night, weren't you?" She glanced at her text message again. "It's not over," Clisty sighed with mixed emotions and a tinge of giddy joy. "I've just been given permission to follow this story to the end. Becca just texted me." Her fingers flew over the touch pad as she typed in out loud, "Yes, Becca. Wow, yes!"

"What's the end gonna' be?" Albert Sinclair asked as he came into the living room from the back of the house. He carried a bundle of sundresses and shorts over his arm.

"Hi Daddy," Clisty paused and gave him a welcome home hug. "The 'end' to Faith's story is as far as we can get, in our efforts at finding where she has been held captive all these years ... and, hopefully, why she was taken?"

"That's quite a task. How long will it take to find the answers do you suppose?" He brushed some stray hair from Clisty's eyes as he had always done.

"I think we can do it—Becca and the team and I. We hope to get more location information from Faith, if she can remember."

"Does she have amnesia?" her dad asked.

"Maybe. I'm no doctor, but, it might be something else, if we could really talk to her. Now, she just answers, 'I don't know,'" Clisty said and then thought for a moment. "When we do get a lead, Jake will go with Becca and I and the camera man to see if we can track them down."

"Jake?" Carol and Al looked at each other with raised eyebrows.

"Okay, okay," she blushed.

"Who's Jake?" her mom asked.

"Detective Jake Davis, Mom. He's with the police department. Laws have been broken."

"You called or texted us almost every day we were in Florida. Why haven't we heard about your detective before this?" Al asked with a stifled grin.

"He's not *my* Detective," Clisty protested, but inside, she remembered she had denied their closeness just yesterday when Becca teased her.

"Why don't you invite him over for dinner later, here with us? You two can strategize on the progress of the story." Carol slapped her knees with both hands like she always did when she had made up her mind about something.

"Mom, you and Daddy just got home. Dad's still cleaning out the car. I will take you two out for dinner." Clisty smiled to herself.

She had finally turned the corner from being a receiver to becoming a giver, and she liked it.

"We do appreciate it, Honey, truly. But, we'd like to visit with you and I really don't want to go back out on the road, not even down to George's Diner or the Coffee Emporium." She sighed as she stood up and took the hanging clothes that Al had brought in from the car.

"Here, Mom, I'll help you with those" Clisty offered. "You take the ones on hangers and I take the folded pieces."

As they walked toward the hall that led to the bedrooms, Al called after them. "It makes me no never mind. You two decide and let me know. I'll get the car-vac going."

As Clisty passed the bathroom door, she slowed and grabbed the door jamb. Her heart began to pound and her breath caught in her throat. "Oh ..." she closed her eyes as she felt her head spin.

"Honey, are you all right?" Carol hurried and dropped the clothes on her bed inside the bedroom and turned back to Clisty. "You don't look so good. Let me help you." She took the clothes that Clisty carried, put her other hand around her daughter's waist and tried to help steady her balance.

"I feel ... so funny," she leaning on the wall just outside her parents' room. She didn't move, hoping the hall would stop swaying like a swinging bridge.

"What happened?" Her mother asked as she helped her into the bedroom and onto the bed. "Lay down a minute, until you feel a little better." After Clisty sat down on the bed, Carol reached down and pulled her daughter's legs onto the covers.

"The bathroom ..." Clisty began but could not finish her thoughts. "I don't know ... something. It felt like I couldn't breathe, like I couldn't take in any more air."

"Oh, Clisty, I am so sorry. I had forgotten how you reacted when they took Faith. It was a terrifying experience for you. They nearly grabbed you right along with her. You fought off that horrible man.

Now, with Faith's return, along with the memories of the home invasion, your reaction to that fearful day has invaded your thoughts again, too." She sat down on the side of the bed beside her daughter and pulled the down-filled duvet across her arms.

"How I reacted when it happened? I don't remember much afterward, just the kidnapping itself. That is burned in my mind." She pulled the cover more tightly around her forearms and closed her eyes. "I remember how his rough, dirty hand felt when he grabbed my arm. It was like a vise that nearly cut off my circulation. And, his foul breathe," she almost gagged as her senses filled with the memory of his odor. "I slipped on the Monopoly game and fell," she began to wring her hands and her lips were so dry, the words stuck in her mouth. "I'm so sorry I didn't put the game away, Mom." She reached up and threw her arms around her mother's neck. "It was my fault. If I hadn't fallen, I could have rescued her."

"Honey, if you hadn't slipped on those cards and fell out of his reach, you would have been taken, too." She patted Clisty's shoulder as she had done for so long. "Try to rest." Her mother let go so Clisty could lay back, touched her hand and held it in her own.

"I can't rest, Mom. I can't remember anything after Faith was gone." Clisty thought out loud. "What happened?"

Carol swallowed hard. She too had tried to forget the tragic events in her own safe home during the few moments she had been gone. "I found you in the bathroom when I got home from the store with the milk. You had curled up into a ball. You were hiding behind the door. When I asked you where Faith was, you said, 'I don't know.'"

"She was here when I left," I reminded you. "Did she go home?" Carol patted Clisty's hand. "Again, you said, 'I don't know.' I didn't know how you could forget such a thing."

"When the police came, you told them about the treasures you and Faith had found when you two were out exploring. You said Faith had a little trouble with her bike chain, but nothing else."

Al came in and placed Carol's hotel one-night-bag on the floor in the corner. "Faith's bicycle was still in the yard when I got home. When I checked it, there was nothin' wrong with the chain or anything else on the bike." He sat down on one of the bedroom chairs and listened.

"Oh Mama, I didn't help the police at all?" Clisty was devastated. "I thought I remembered that I gave them valuable information."

"You did," her mother assured her as she smiled. "They said you were repressing the memory of the kidnapping, so they called in a psychologist to talk to you."

"Dr. Phillips," her dad added.

"Did the psychologist help me remember?" Her eyes blinked and she squinted as if she were trying to see into a past long forgotten.

"Yes, the repression was there but she helped you anyway. Since you were a minor, your dad and I sat in the corner of the room when she interviewed you. We had our lawyer with us. They treated the interview like a deposition, recorded it and then they transcribed the recording."

Al reached into the dresser drawer beside him, sorted through the gold covered, jewelry gift boxes and pulled some papers from the bottom. He handed the few sheets of paper to his wife.

Carol took the legal size type written papers and smoothed out the fold lines with her hands. "This is the transcript of the interview. We saved it all of these years. That was such a difficult time for all of us."

"Read what it says, Mom. I have to know."

Carol lifted her reading glasses that hung from the chain around her neck and put them to her eyes. At first she hesitated and then began to read the dialog printed by the court.

Transcript of the eye witness account of Clisty Sinclair, age 9:

Dr. Yvonne Phillips: "Hi Clisty. What can you tell us about the man who kidnapped your friend, Faith? It was a man, wasn't it?"

Clisty Sinclair: "I don't know what you mean."

Carol placed the paper in her lap for a moment. "Dr. Phillips tried to reach your memory using a normal interview method. She quickly saw that wouldn't work, so she began in a different way."

Dr. Yvonne Phillips: Someone stopped by your house to pick up a package, didn't they? Was the person a stranger?"

Clisty Sinclair: "What did you say? There wasn't any package."

Dr. Yvonne Phillips: "The package was wrapped in pink ribbon, Honey. It was a sweet package."

Clisty Sinclair: "I didn't like him."

Dr. Yvonne Phillips: "Why didn't you like him? Was he mean?"

Clisty Sinclair: "He nearly broke the package he was supposed to pick up."

Dr. Yvonne Phillips: "Did he put the package in the basket of his bicycle, like you and Faith do when you ride?"

Clisty Sinclair: "No, he had an old truck."

Dr. Yvonne Phillips: "Oh, a truck. How do you know it was a truck if you were hiding?"

Clisty Sinclair: "'Cause it sounded like Grandpa's truck and Grandpa said his truck made such a racket because it was as old as he was."

Dr. Yvonne Phillips: "That's good, Clisty. I'll bet the man said nothing about where he was taking the package."

Clisty Sinclair: "He said if the package didn't stop making so much noise, he's drop it in the lake, 'cause he'd drive right down Michigan Avenue."

Dr. Yvonne Phillips: "So you know where Faith was taken?"

Clisty Sinclair: "What? I don't know what you mean. I just heard him yelling about driving a hundred-sixty miles away, no one would look for the pink package in another state."

Carol looked up from the paper and added, "Then you began to cry. When she started to walk out of the room, you whispered to her, 'He'll come back for me. I have to hide again.' She told me that you gave them a lot of information that they needed, information they didn't already have. Before she left the room, she told us that you were repressing all the bad memories because they were too frightening for you to remember."

"But, I did remember a little when she didn't ask me directly?"

"That's right. She asked in such a way that you corrected her seeming misperceptions, which gave them a little information. After she talked to you, they realized that the man took Faith into Illinois, maybe to the Chicago area. They would never have found that out any other way."

Albert had been listening, shook his head and then changed the subject. He must have heard all he could hear. "So, what's the plan about food, you two? I'd like to eat early, so I can go to bed equally early."

"We'll think about dinner in a minute, Al," Carol got him back on track and stood up. Tears gathered in her eyes as she turned to Clisty. "You had nightmares for months after Faith disappeared. Actually, as frightening as those terrible dreams were, they helped you remember what you had protected yourself from. That's why the memories are so vivid to you now and that's why you healed after a time. Faith has lived through it every day. She has never started healing because she has never stopped living it."

"Then, I know how Faith feels, Mom." Clisty swung her legs to the side of the bed and stood up. "I feel better now. I'll call Jake and he can come over after his shift." She thought for a moment and added, "Faith doesn't have amnesia, Mom. She's suffering from the same crippling fear I felt on that terrible day when he stole her. And, we know where she was taken."

• • • • •

The doorbell rang around 4:30 at the Sinclair home. They had gathered in the living room to decide about food. Clisty hurried to the door and looked through the beveled glass. Although the prisms distorted the image with a rainbow of colors, Clisty recognized Jake Davis's face as he waited on the porch.

"Wow," she swooned when she opened the door, "that smells wonderful." He carried a bucket of original crust chicken with potato wedges, green beans and yummy smelling biscuits into the house. In the other hand was a small pie; and a package of soft drinks was tucked under his arm. "Jake, how wonderful!" She gasped as she inhaled the perfume of the Colonel.

"Jake?" both Al and Carol perked up at the same time.

"Mom, Dad," Clisty began as she took the chicken and placed the bucket on the table. "This is Detective Jake Davis and we have solved our dinner dilemma. Jake is treating and we don't have to go out. And ... just for you, Dad, we can eat early. We'll be out of your hair by 6 pm for sure."

Albert Sinclair's smile nearly spilled off his face as he jumped up and offered his hand. "Detective," he squared his shoulders, "I am so happy to meet you. We have heard absolutely nothing about you."

"Dad!" Clisty blushed and everyone laughed. They all shared great pats on the back and robust handshakes.

Jake looked at Clisty and shrugged. "All I've heard about you two is that you were smart enough to get out of our weather and spend your winter in Florida. What I want to know is how did a young man like you manage to retire so early?"

"Retire?" Al questioned.

67

"If you're not retired, how were you able to spend two months in Florida?" Jake questioned as he removed the cardboard lid from the bucket.

"I had a month's vacation; that was March. Then, winter decided to stick around up here. I'm the purchasing agent for Bontrager Manufacturing. Walt Bontrager told me to stay where it was warm and work from my laptop down there."

"Maybe you can convince the boss of that next year, too," Jake suggested as he slipped his arm around Clisty's waste.

Carol smiled as she watched the new couple together. "We hoped that Clisty would finally get away from her work and sterile apartment, come down and stick her toes in the sand; but, it didn't happen."

"Okay, okay," Clisty halted the jabs as she raised her hands in a time-out signal. As the laughter settled like warm gravy dripping over potatoes, she added, "I'm glad my three favorite people have finally met, especially when another long lost friend has found her way home."

Part III
Backstory - 1

"How do you want to set up this first interview with Faith, Becca?" Clisty asked as she studied the room. "It's my apartment, but you're the director. Hopefully, she'll feel more relaxed here in my home."

"First of all, do you think Faith will drink coffee? I'll put some on before she and her parents get here. That could settle things down and make her feel at home. The taping of this first segment will probably be the hardest."

"Coffee? Sure. If she doesn't want any, I know I will," Clisty flicked a little nothing fuzz off the table.

"Do you want to place those two blue Edwardian wingback chairs in front of the fireplace, facing each other?" Becca asked as she looked around and studied the room.

"Maybe," Clisty thought as she started moving the one nearest to her. "I don't know, Becca," she said as she thought about the placement.

"What's wrong?" Becca paused. "I know we moved the chairs from their assigned spots. You probably measured the distance from the couch and positioned them at a precise angle."

"Don't laugh," Clisty said sheepishly.

"On, no, Clisty, you didn't?" She threw her hands to her hips and laughed. "I knew you like minimal décor but I didn't know you took it to a compulsive level."

"Becca, don't be silly. I ..." Clisty protested as she pushed the chair in front of her at an odd angle. "There, is that better?"

"It doesn't bother me," Becca threw up both hands. "The question is, does it bother you?"

"I'm not going to worry about it. You put the chairs wherever you want them," she laughed. The coffee table was a huge square tufted leather piece in dark blue. "I know the usual setup for a TV interview is face-to-face with nothing between you." Clisty stood beside the table/footrest and studied it for a moment. "I'm afraid Faith is going to want to hide, to protect herself." Her eyes darted back and forth as she checked the possibilities. "What if we put the coffee table between us, but just a little off center? It will give her a place to put her coffee cup and provide some separation between us."

"That is brilliant." Becca started to pull the leather piece toward the chairs. "Wait," she pointed to the ottoman coffee table, "I don't want to scratch the floors. You pick up one end."

"I'm sure it won't hurt anything," Clisty shrugged as she picked up the end of the ottoman. "I'll get out some nice cups and saucers and a tray so the whole thing will balance on the footstool, while you set the stage, so to speak."

The doorbell rang as Becca started the coffee. "They're early," Becca gasped.

"No, I'll bet that's Clint with the camera. Let's hope. Faith may become anxious if things are still being set up," Clisty agreed. She hurried to the door.

Clint carried the TV camera in one hand and an equipment bag in the other and plopped them on the floor behind the couch. "That's an interesting set up," he nodded toward the chairs and coffee table. "Open and closed at the same time. That should make her feel more comfortable."

Everyone connected with Faith's story knew her background. Long tall Clint would be the one to film the entire process, from Fort Wayne and west into Illinois, maybe Chicago.

The doorbell rang again and the show was on. From the moment Faith walked into the house, the focus had to be on putting her at ease while dragging the most horrid memories out of her fragile memory. Her parents came with her.

"It's good to see you again," Roma said as she gave Clisty a hug.

"Clisty," Ralph nodded in her direction."

"Thank you for coming Mr. and Mrs. Sterling," Becca began. "I'm sure Faith will feel more comfortable with you two here."

"We had to bring her. She can't drive," Ralph explained as he shook his head. "There are so many things she can't comprehend. Not because she isn't intelligent," he whispered. "She is." He kept shaking his head in disbelief. "Like, she hadn't seen a traffic light before her trip home. She said she had figured that drivers stop on red and go on green." His eyes glazed over with tears. "What has she been through?"

"We're going to find out, I hope," Clisty looked over at Faith and smiled sympathetically. Faith looked beautiful, although still weak and unsure of herself. "How do you feel, Faith?" Clisty asked as she hugged her old friend and took her jacket.

"It seemed like spring was late when we first got to Indiana, but now the trees are beginning to bloom and the tulips are popping up a little. It's only been a week since ... Pooky and I went into the hospital."

"Speaking of Pooky, my mom was thrilled to watch her today. You have quite a daughter. You are a good mother," Clisty kept talking as she ushered Faith over to the two facing chairs. "She took to my mom like a second grandma."

When the doorbell rang a third time, Becca went to the door so as not to break the rapport Clisty was beginning to build. "Hi Jake," Becca grabbed his sleeve and pulled him into the apartment. "We're already setting the mood in here. Go slow with Faith."

"Don't worry, I'm here only to observe." He walked over toward the facing chairs and stopped near the couch. "Hi Faith, it's good to see you again."

"Again?" Faith's body recoiled from Jake's presence.

"I came to the hospital several times," he said slowly. "Is it okay if I sit here on the sofa?"

"Okay? I guess," Faith stammered.

"Do you remember my friend, Detective Jake Davis of the Fort Wayne police department?" Clisty asked.

"Maybe," she smiled faintly then looked around the apartment. "You have a lovely home, Clisty." Her blue eyes searched every inch of her surroundings, "It's so clean." When her eyes came to rest on the fireplace mantle, her eyes sparkled. "Your prayer angel," she sighed with a smile.

"You remember my angel?" Clisty asked with joy in her voice. "Faith," she paused not wanting to rush her, "we would like to film these conversations. Do you remember what we talked about the other day?"

"About what?" She began twisting a tissue she pulled from her pocket until it began to fall in tiny shreds to the floor.

"Would you like a cup of coffee, Faith?" Becca asked as she poured a cup. "Maybe a cookie to go with it?"

Faith's eyes shifted from Becca to her mother. "Mama brought cookies to the hospital. I'm not allowed to have sweets."

"Really?" Clisty asked, and then looked at Clint to see if he was ready to film. He gave a thumbs-up and Clisty continued. "Who told you not to eat sweets?" Then to Becca she added, "Coffee would be great for both of us, and, I know I'd enjoy a cookie."

Becca brought the hot brew and a small platter of shortbread cookies she had brought in. "Here you are Faith and the pot is full. Roma, Ralph, would you two like some?"

"No thank you," Roma waved her hand away.

"Yes, please. Maybe it will clear my head," Ralph agreed.

After a quick break of coffee and cookies, Clisty tried again to make a connection. "You said you liked the flowers. There were always beautiful, large flower beds in Swinney Park. The blossoms were so fragrant; it smelled like perfume was always in the air."

"Yes ..." Faith closed her eyes as a soft, sweet smile crossed her face. "I can smell them." Quickly, her eyes popped open, large and frightened. "I'm not supposed to day dream."

"You're not allowed to eat sweets, or pause and remember? Faith, who gave you those rules?"

"They did, of course, The Guardians."

Clisty looked at Jake and the Sterlings. "The Guardians? Who are The Guardians?"

"My family."

Roma Sterling's eyes flashed open wide. Ralph scooted to the edge of the couch cushion.

"Their name was Guardian?" Clisty asked and wondered if it all had been too easy.

"No. That's what they were, not who they were." Her coffee cup rattled in her hand so she placed it on the ottoman. With her eyes cast down, she explained. "He said, since my parents sold me to them, I was their slave. But, if I was good, he would treat me like a daughter. He said he was my guardian. So, I tried to be really good, no sweets so they didn't have to spend money on dentists, no day dreaming because that would make me a lazy worker."

"Is that the way they treated you, the way your life went the whole time you were with them?" Clisty asked as the camera kept rolling.

"With him, yes. I could never call him by name. But, I called her, Lady. Lady would come into my room and read to me. She taught me all the subjects of school. She would brush my hair. Their son, Steven went to school. When I married Steven, I was seventeen and he was twenty. He showed me love and gentleness."

"Where did you and Steven live, Faith?" Clisty paused and waited patiently. She hoped she was not pushing her friend.

"In our rooms, of course. We used Steven's old room as our bedroom and my room as a sitting room. There was a bathroom off my room. The Guardian helped Steven put a door between the bedroom and sitting room so it was like a little apartment. After Pooky was born, they gave us another small bedroom to use as a nursery. Sometimes, we ate our meals with Lady and The Guardian, but not very often." There was a softening in Faith's words.

"Did ... the man ever hurt you?" Clisty again waited. She didn't want to lead her friend or coach her in any way. There could be no contamination, no recovery of repressed memories due to guided suggestions.

"Hurt me?" Faith's eye lids fluttered and her voice faded. "I don't know what you mean."

"Did he touch you in ways that made you feel uncomfortable, as a child or any time?" Clisty's tone was empathetic. She didn't want to embarrass her or cause her to pull away emotionally.

"After he grabbed me in your living room and then dragged me in the house once we were at home, he never touched me again, except to hit me. The only time he talked to me was to yell rules and bawl me out." Faith's expression seemed to wilt, like a beautiful flower that hadn't had enough life-giving water.

"Did ... the lady, ever hurt you?"

"Lady? No, not like hitting me or anything. She just left me all alone so much. Not 'cause she wanted to. She treated me like her daughter when she was allowed to spend time with me." Tears started to flow down her cheeks. "I was so utterly alone most of the time."

"What about Steven? Did you two talk or play games or anything? Did he spend time with you?"

"The Guardian wouldn't let him be alone with me." Faith looked into the fireplace that burned with a soft glow.

"Then how ...?" Clisty started then stopped and let Faith fill in the rest of it.

"The Guardian locked my bedroom door every night. As I got older, and he saw that I didn't leave my room, he stopped locking it. With no locked door between us, Steven would creep into my room at night and we'd just talk."

Clisty wondered if Faith was ready for the next question but she had to ask. "Did you and Steven get sexually involved? Is that why you were allowed to marry?"

"No ... no!" Faith shrunk back as she denied sexual encounters. "Finally, when I was seventeen, Steven asked his father if we could be married." She closed her eyes again. Her shoulders relaxed and she smiled.

"Do you see those sweet memories, Faith?" Clisty asked as she watched her friend's face fill with joy. "Memories of your marriage and the love Steven had for you?"

"Yes" she whispered.

Clisty leaned forward and tried to breathe trust and love into the space that remained between them. "If you never went outside, and you never saw anyone, who married you and Steven?"

"The Guardian, of course. He's the Head Master of the Freedom Temple. All the slaves obey The Guardian, even when he's mean and abusive." Faith's sweet expression changed back to the flat, marionette face of one who never thought for herself, she only obeyed. "He cleaned himself up and had his teeth fixed and turned himself into a Head Master." From somewhere deep within her, she began to repeat in rapid fire delivery, a pledge of allegiance by rote memory. "The Head Master is kind and good, full of wisdom and love. He is all knowing. He is the voice of God."

Clisty was stunned. How could she get Faith to give more details of her background if some questions caused her to slip into a robotic daze? She hoped that recent memories would be easier to recall than distant ones.

"Faith," Clisty started a new line of questioning and placed her hand on her friend's knee. She tried to anchor Faith to the present with her touch. "Faith, let's talk about the other day, with the bank robber, Melvin Dean Fargo."

Faith blinked several times and looked at Clisty. "Okay."

"How did you get away from Fargo, and then end up back at the house on North Gramercy again?" Clisty waited and watched Faith try to recount what had happened only days before.

"He said he was going to go to the bank and Pooky and I had to go with him so we wouldn't escape." Her gaze searched the area in the upper right edge of her memory. "We had no idea that he was going to rob it."

"Where were you when he threatened the teller?" Clisty asked, hoping Faith was not an unplanned accomplice to a robbery.

"He kept his right hand in his pocket and held my arm with his left. He ordered me to hold on to Pooky." Suddenly her eyes flashed with fear. "Then, Clisty, he pulled a gun out of his pocket and ordered a teller to give him all the money." Faith put her hands to her face and covered her eyes.

"You must have been terrified," Clisty whispered. "Where was Pooky?"

"She was still beside me. When Fargo looked at the money the teller was putting in a bag, he released his grip on me. I grabbed Pooky and we ran out. I told her to find the shop we saw you go in on our way to the bank. I would escape and try to get Fargo to follow me and not her."

"You had seen me earlier?" Clisty asked, amazed at all the interconnected miracles of seeming happenstance.

"I had seen your news program on TV when we first arrived on Gramercy and I recognized you right away. When I saw you go in the shop late in the afternoon, I noticed it was just down the street from your parents' house."

"You have quite a memory." Clisty gathered up the threads of the conversation and pulled Faith back to her escape from Fargo. "So, you sent Pooky away, hoping she could find the coffee shop. How did you feel when you saw her run out on her own?"

"I was so afraid but, she had to get as far from Fargo as possible. Then, I ran to the side when I saw Fargo race out the door. He passed right behind me. I guess he didn't think I'd stop just outside the bank."

"We all saw you, Faith, on the surveillance camera. Fargo had on a dark blue hoodie, didn't he?" Clisty asked.

"Yes. You said you saw me on some kind of camera?" she asked and smiled.

"We'll talk about surveillance cameras some other time," Clisty assured her. "What happened next?"

"Then, I ran off and tried to find the coffee shop and Pooky. At first, I tried to make sure Fargo would see and follow me, so Pooky would have a head start." Faith drank from her cup, touched the cookie and then put it down.

"Faith," Clisty reached for her hand, "you were so brave."

"I didn't feel brave. I just ran. I darted down streets, across lawns and back alleys. I thought I had gotten away from him. It got dark but I could still recognize parts of the old neighborhood. Then I saw your parents' house but no one was home. It was all dark."

Clisty gasped in validation. "I thought you were in the yard."

Faith looked over at Becca. "I saw Fargo knock you down and I panicked. I picked up a broken branch and swung it at him." Her arms and whole body acted out the attack again. "I know I hit him, but I didn't know if I had stopped him, so I started to run." She looked out the window across the room and sighed deeply.

"Then what happened, Faith?" Clisty leaned toward her friend. Behind the camera, Roma held a tissue to her mouth and muffling the frequent gasps that escaped.

"I only managed to get a few houses down the street from your mom and dad's when Fargo caught up to me." Her hands trembled as she shifted in her chair. "He grabbed me by my hair. 'Where is she?' he yelled. I told him I didn't know where Pooky was. He dragged me to the truck and shoved me in." She stopped and looked back at her dad. "Daddy, I was a prisoner again and I just wanted to come home."

III

Backstory - 2

"Monday always comes when it's not wanted," Clisty moaned to Becca, with her cell phone set on *speaker*.

"I know. I know, but just think of some of the reasons why you would have to sleep all the time: recovery from the plague; really advanced old age; you have narcolepsy and you fall asleep on the creepy guy next to you on the bus; you died and were laid to rest last week; do I need to go on?" Becca quipped.

"I wonder, if I died what would my Heavenly job be?" she yawned. "I might be a cloud-comfort-tester. Then again, I'd probably chase rebellious cherubs all over the golden streets, so I can interview them and ask the age old question, "Why do you rebel?"

"Oh bother," Becca laughed. "Maybe I'd have to direct that bunch of kids with the wings."

"Becca, that's it. Kids! What is it that Pooky told us? 'Daddy said I could go to school but then Grandpa said no.'" Clisty raked her hand through her hair and looked in the mirror. "Oh Becca, I look awful. I'm glad that skype hasn't come to the cell phone industry yet—at least not to mine."

"I told you to cover all the looking glasses in your apartment in black fabric and not pull them down until at least, uh, two in the afternoon. Before mid-afternoon, you're only looking at the ghost of the previous night."

"I'll try to remember that." Clisty started to pace along the carpet runner beside her bed. "Let's get back to Pooky. Becca, the child may remember more than Faith does, especially if she was given a little more freedom, like her two weeks in school."

"You call the Sterlings and I'll get ready and meet you there." Becca suggested.

"Wait until I've had a chance to sit down with them. I don't want to run in there with lights and camera blazing." That settled it. "I'll call you after I talk to them."

Clisty jumped out of her night clothes and into the shower. *I hope this works.* While the hot water peppered her body from the multiple jets, she started planning her strategy. Later, dressed in her new black spring-weight suit she had bought before the events of Friday had turned her world upside down, she hurried out to her car.

• • • • •

"Good Morning, Clisty," Roma said as she opened the front door. "Come in." She led the way through the living room. "Have you had your coffee yet this morning?"

"Just one cup. I'm ready for my second one," she chuckled as she followed Roma into the kitchen.

"Let's sit down here a minute." Roma pointed to the ladder-back chairs that sat around the kitchen table. "Toast?"

"No thanks, Roma." She reached for the sugar and stirred in a spoonful. "I was hoping to talk to Pooky this morning. What do you think? Will she talk to me?"

"Faith has wanted Pooky to stay in the background, out of the camera lights. I'm sure you can't blame her."

"Not at all," Clisty agreed, and she did, but there were other issues at play. "Since Pooky was out in the world more than Faith, there may be someone who would recognize her. While they may be a friendly neighbor, they could also be the evil ones who kept Pooky in the house with Faith all those years. We all have to keep her safe."

"That's what I mean," Roma agreed. "She is relaxing more and letting Ralph and I get closer to her. At first, she was so open with me. Although, it's harder for Pooky to get near her grandpa. Literally. She talks to him now, but from a distance." She shook her head in disbelief. "I can't believe we have Faith home. I can't believe a wonderful granddaughter came with her. I can't believe that Faith was held as a strange slave for eighteen years."

"I know," Clisty admitted. "She didn't have to work for them; she just ... filled some role, I guess. I think her job was to be the lady's daughter, but The Guardian couldn't let go of his power as supreme ... what did she call him ... Head Master?" The coffee was still hot so Clisty sipped carefully. "Of course, I wouldn't put Pooky on the news. Just talk."

"I'll have to ask Faith and she's still sleeping." Roma picked up the coffee pot, and then put it back on the warming burner. "She sleeps so much, Clisty."

"That's been her way of healing her mind and body, Roma. She seems to have slept a lot over the last eighteen years. If she were awake all day, she would realize how alone she was ... for hours and hours. Those who are depressed, sleep a lot."

"She did say she was allowed to read and she enjoyed that. Reading gave her some contact with the world around her. Not just books, the lady let her read magazines when The Guardian wasn't around."

"Can you just imagine all the places Faith has been within the pages of her books and magazines?" Clisty thought for a minute. "I wonder how she could pronounce all the words. She was all alone in her room most of the time."

"She probably just put her own sounds and meaning to the words. That's what my grandfather did." Roma smiled the smile of happy memories. "Grandpa Georgie was a self-made man. He read everything he could lay his hands on. We sometimes had to figure out what he was talking about when he was trying to explain something he had read, because his pronunciation was so bad, but we all admired his knowledge. Knowledge isn't pronunciation, Clisty; it's investigation, inquisitiveness."

"I like that, Roma." She paused and thought about all that Roma had said. "I want to investigate. I want to find out why that man took Faith, where he took her and what her life was like. And ..." again she paused to think if she was ready to tell anyone about her new career offer, "I've been given a great opportunity."

"Can you tell me about it, Clisty? Maybe you want to talk about it?"

"It's yes to both. But, there's someone I need to tell first." She had made up her mind. She had to find Jake.

• • • • •

Officer Jeremy Rhodes jumped to his feet when Clisty walked into the police station later. "Miss Sinclair—"

"It's Clisty, remember, Jeremy?" she said as she smiled.

"Yes, Ma'am ... Clisty. I'm sorry Ma'am. I watch you on the news every evening and it just seems like I'm talking to a celebrity."

"If I ever become a celebrity, I will be forced to resign. I wouldn't be able to stand to look at myself in the mirror. Come to think of it, someone told me a mirror shouldn't be looked into before noon anyway."

"I think I understand that rule." He winked and rubbed his chin. "Is there anything I can do for you?"

"Is Jake in?" She looked around the room of desks and chairs, all lined up, yet working together.

"Did I hear my name?" Jake asked as he came out of a separate office. "Hi, Babe." His smile was large and matched the spark in his eyes. "What brings you down here?"

"I have to talk to you," she said as she walked over to him, took his elbow and directed him back into his private office. She could feel all the eyes in the department following them. Even with the door closed, the glass in the window and in the door made her feel like she was in a glass bowl. She laughed to herself. "Men do like their aquariums."

"Is there something wrong?" he asked. His brow furrowed with concern or curiosity, Clisty wasn't sure which.

"So many things, Jake." She fumbled with the oversized gray buttons on her red coat. Finally, Jake took her hands and placed them at her sides. He drew so close she could hear his breathing. As her coat fell from her shoulders, she could hear a collective sigh from beyond the windows, while Jake placed the coat on a chair. The room was full of unspoken words, but Clisty knew there were words that she had to say. She didn't know why her hands were shaking but she had to get through all the connected pieces of her life.

"Jake," she pointed toward the desk, "you sit there and I'll sit here." While she sat on one of the facing chairs, she barely perched on the edge. Jake leaned back on the desk and waited, his arms folded across this chest.

"First, it occurred to me that Pooky has lived in the same house, the same neighborhood, the same town as Faith has lived since she was born eight years ago. Maybe she can remember something, names, streets, even what town they lived in."

Jake leaned in closer with the new possibilities. "Will Pooky talk if I'm in the room with you?"

"I think that will be okay. You were with us when we first met her and she was comfortable with you then, although her trust does fluctuate." She looked down at her fingernails; then she hid them in her pockets. "The other thing is ... I have been given the go-ahead to chase this story as far as it goes. That will probably mean, at least, leaving the state, probably going to Illinois. Can you ..." she hesitated. She didn't want Jake to think she was being forward. "Do you think your department would let you go with us: Becca and Clint and me?"

Jake's eyes brightened; the corners of his mouth turned up into a boyish grin. "You're asking me to go to Illinois with you?"

"Jake, now, cut it out," she blushed. "I'm asking if the Police Department wants to send someone with us as we gather information about an unsolved kidnapping." In her embarrassment, she stood up and focused her eyes on the budding spring day beyond the window.

"Oh," he drew out, "if that's what you're asking, then yeah, they will probable send me." Jake reached out, turned her around so he could see her, and wrapped his arms around her. "That's great. I'm glad the station is letting you pursue the story." He leaned back and looked into her eyes.

She wondered if he saw the rest of the story. "It's not just the station, Jake. It's the network. They're talking about putting it on the national news, like a spot on their Tuesday night news magazine."

"Clisty, that is great! It could really advance your career," he glanced at the other windows that formed the glass wall to the outer office. "A kiss right now would be most appropriate, but perhaps all the eyes ..."

Clisty stood up, placed her hands on both sides of Jake's face, pulled him close and kissed him with genuine tenderness. Looking at him, she added, "I agree, most appropriate ... and a little inappropriate. At least no one can accuse me of work place harassment. I don't work here." She pressed her forehead into Jake's chest. "But ... maybe not the best timing ... or perhaps it is."

"I don't know what you're talking about, but ... I think, I'm willing to listen." He lifted her hands and kissed them tenderly.

"The kiss may have been an effort to soften you up before my last point," she admitted. "My career may have already been boosted." She turned and looked out the window again onto early pale green shoots. "If the story goes well, the network is offering me a spot on their National, New York based, News Magazine. They'll call it, *Stories from the Heartland*. They want to offer positive stories of victory over adversity from real people who live and work in the middle of the country, away from Broadway and Rodeo Drive."

"Babe, that's wonderful." He threw his head back and exhaled from his toes. "Wait," he stopped and jerked his eyes back to Clisty. "You just said New York based."

"That's right. The program is a network show, based in New York City." She turned to face him. "But, we can ..."

"Thank goodness, for a minute I didn't know if there would be a, *we can* anything in there."

· · · · ·

"We are continuing our expanded story of the suspected bank robber and his hostage," Clisty updated the viewers that evening on the eleven o'clock news.

Dan Drummond faced the camera. "Melvin Dean Fargo, who was apprehended by police following last Friday's stand-off, is charged with Criminal Confinement. His hostage? The woman believed to be the witness in Friday's bank robbery." They did not re-run the news clip from the ATM.

Clisty continued in confidence as her back straightened even more. "The network wants this newscaster to investigate Mr. Fargo, even beyond any involvement he may or may not have in the robbery at the bank. Our investigation goes far beyond those questions. It is our promise, to pursue this case until we answer all questions. And, that is the News at Eleven."

III

Backstory - 3

"It's great to see you looking so good," Clisty stood back and held the door to WFT-TV.

"Hi Clisty," Faith hugged her friend and stepped into the reception area of the TV station. "I'm feeling a little better."

"Roma and Ralph, come in. We'll make room for everyone." Becca directed them to the chairs and took their jackets. "Jake Davis is coming too. Brenda, our receptionist, will watch for him."

"Oh, I didn't know," Faith recoiled emotionally.

"It'll be okay, Faith. You and I talked about it yesterday when I stopped by your parents' home," Clisty reminded her. Then she turned, "Hi Pooky." She took the time to hug Faith's daughter, hoping Faith would have enough time and space to remember their conversation.

Roma reminded her softly. "We all sat around the table, Faith, remember?"

"Let's go into the studio and look it over. It's just a room with special equipment in it." Clisty led the way, through the news room and into the studio.

"Maybe," Faith's voice trailed off as she stared with wide eyes around the room.

"I know it must look very foreign to you, but it's really just a work room, like the kitchen in your home. We make TV news programs in here, and you prepare food in your kitchen."

"Where is the microphone and camera?" Pooky asked as she stepped out of the background and into light.

"The mic is there on the news desk." Clisty pointed.

"But we—" Becca started.

"Aren't quite ready for that stuff," Clisty jumped in. She knew Faith didn't want Pooky's picture out in the public so they would take that slowly. On the other hand, Jake would need the interview on film so there could be no question about the process later. Pooky could not appear to say things she would not have said on her own.

"Faith," Clisty pointed to the large, floor-camera, "Clint can film Pooky on this camera, strictly for police use. We won't broadcast it into viewers' homes. Or, he can use the shoulder camera if you think Pooky would be frightened by the big one." She hoped if she gave Faith a choice, she may feel less vulnerable.

Faith's shoulders dropped and her eyes shifted to the floor. "Maybe we'll not film it at all," her words tumbled out of her mouth in rapid succession. "What's important is what she says, not what she looks like."

"That's right. You're absolutely correct," Jake added as he came into the studio. He stopped just a few feet inside the door so Faith and Pooky wouldn't feel cornered. "The choice is yours, Faith. You're the mom. It's just that ..." he paused, slipped into the room and leaned casually on the wall. "If you decide not to have her filmed at all, when we catch your kidnapper, his lawyer could claim that we put the words in Pooky's mouth. With the film, we can prove she said it all on her own. What do you think?" He paused and gave Faith time for the choices to catch up to her.

"Faith, I told you about my telling your story, using your words and Pooky's memories too, on a news magazine. Maybe there'll be something in the story that will help another child stay safe from a kidnapper."

Faith looked at her daughter. Her sad eyes studied the cherished face.

"Please Mama, please," Pooky steepled her fingers into a prayer and jumped up and down.

Clisty saw Faith smile, something she had not witnessed since they were both children. Her heart warmed. "I will do the interview myself. Jake is here only to take his own notes. As we take breaks from time to time, he may offer some questions I had not thought about. Does that seem reasonable to you?"

"Faith," Roma said softly, "it sounds to me like Pooky will be even safer if they can find the kidnapper."

"The Guardian won't be found."

"Why do you say that?" Clisty asked. "We have to be positive."

"I am, Clisty. I am positive you will not find him. He told me he wouldn't be found, what seems like, every day of my life." Her voice dropped off and she appeared to shudder, like a reptile had slithered across her path.

"He told you lots of things, Faith, like you said, every day of your life. He probably said, 'You'll never get away,' didn't he?"

Faith's eyes brighten, a positive sign Clisty had not yet seen. "He said it nearly every day, at least for the first ten or twelve years of my slavery."

"I hate that word, Faith," her mother set her jaw.

"I hate that life," Faith answered, a little stronger than before.

"Hey, I thought this was about me," Pooky insisted.

"You are absolutely right, Honey," Becca agreed. "I'm going to be your producer-director, so ... let's place you on the interview set here, face to face with Clisty."

"But, where's the microphone?" Pooky asked as she studied the cluster of chairs.

"Right here," Becca pointed to the little clips she held in her hand. "You won't be at the news desk, with all the equipment over there. Both you and Clisty will clip a tiny microphone onto your clothes. You can move around and we can still pick up your voice."

"Well ... okay," she said as she scooted back into one of the side chairs.

As Clisty took her seat facing Pooky, she attached her lapel mic. "Hi Pooky. It now occurred to me that I don't know your last name."

"What do you mean?" Pooky's eyes blinked and she said no more.

"I'm Clisty Sinclair. I have a first name, Clisty and a second name, Sinclair. Your first name is Pooky. What is your last name?"

"I don't have another name."

Clisty stopped. She lost her next question, but gathered her thoughts again quickly. "Your daddy's first name is Steven. What was his last name?"

"I don't know." Pooky looked over at her mother and shrugged.

"Steven had no last name," Faith answered in a flat tone, as if last names were rare.

"You said he went to school," Clisty continued to question Faith where she sat off camera.

"He used the last name, Jones. But, that wasn't his real second name." Faith seemed to chill for a moment. "No one was to speak the name of The Guardian."

"So, did you use the name, Pooky Jones, when you were in school?" Clisty asked.

"Yes, Pooky Jones," she remembered. "But, I wasn't in school very long," she said as she leaned her chin in her hand on the chair rest. Her expression had slipped into a pout.

"You told me about school. Do you want to tell the people about school?"

"I played Red Riding Hood in the school play. Daddy said I could go to school, but when Grandpa found out, he said I had to quit." She shook her head in disbelief. "Why did he have to find out?"

"Do you know who told him you were going to school?" Clisty asked. "Where was your grandfather during the daytime?"

"He was at work." Pooky swung her feet back and forth.

"Work? Where did he work?"

Pooky looked at her in disbelief. "I already told you. He's the Head Master of the Freedom Temple."

"That's right, you did tell me," Clisty admitted, allowing the child to have the superior hand. "I guess I forgot." She slowed down and looked away, sneaking up on the next question from the side. "Your mother told me that The Guardian smelled bad." She looked back at Pooky, like someone in need of help. "How could a leader in an organization ... stink?"

"He wasn't supposed to eat cookies or candy. When he did, he'd act funny, sweat and stink."

"Did you hear Grandma warn him about sugar diabetes?"

"Yeah, that was the word."

"So, he worked at the Freedom Temple? What is the Freedom Temple?" Clisty asked, careful to use low, non-demanding tones.

"It's like a church, Grandma said."

"Didn't you ever go to that church?" Clisty tried not to shake her head. Everything Pooky told her sounded preposterous. A smelly, swearing, evil man who would kidnap a child and hold her as a slave, was the spiritual leader of a congregation?

"Grandma said no one was to know that Mama was Daddy's sister. So, Daddy went to the Temple on Friday night, but not Mama or me. She said, Grandpa brought Mama home for her, to be Grandma's little girl and then, when she was old enough, she'd be Daddy's wife."

"Wow," Clisty exhaled slowly. "You remember all those relationships?" She felt sick inside. The Guardian planned Faith's life even before he took her. Then, he controlled her so it would all work out as he planned.

"Sure," Pooky said. "I had to remember about Mama and Daddy. We rehearsed it like my part in the play. Grandpa said I had to always remember, 'cause if I didn't he could lose Mama and me."

Clisty smiled to reassure her. "You have a very good memory. Do you know why your grandfather took you out of school after your daddy said you could go?"

"It was my teacher's fault," she pouted some more. "She said she had to make a home-visit to all the kid's homes in her class. She'd already gone to the other kids' houses 'cause they had started school before me. Grandpa said she couldn't come to our house and pulled me out of school."

"I bet you miss the friends you made at school," Clisty said as she remembered the wonderful times she had with Faith as a child. Her heart ached for Pooky and her lonely life.

"There was one girl. Her name was Leenie. She was my dearest friend," her words seemed to drift off to a memory that hid from her grandfather in a secret corner of her mind. "In the afternoon, I would sit by the front window, behind the curtain I could see through, and listen to the kids as they laughed and played on their way home from school." Tears slipped down her face and she brushed them away with her sleeve.

"I'm glad you had a friend, even if you couldn't keep her."

"Oh, I kept her," she perked up. "She would leave a note for me under a rock near the end of our sidewalk. I'd sneak out at night and get it and leave a note for her." Pooky turned up her chin in defiant satisfaction, folded her arms and sat back.

"That sounds like a dangerous system. What if you were caught?"

"I never was," Pooky turned her head back and forth in an exaggerated *no*. "She'd tell me what she did at school during the day. Then, she'd sign it, Leenie Lambert, 1221 W. Benton Avenue."

"You have a really good memory, Pooky." Clisty's pulse raced. Would she be able to get the information she needed? "Can you remember anything else?"

"I remembered the school's nickname, something about a big dog."

"Those are good words to remember, Pooky," Clisty said as she reached over and patted Pooky's knee. "I was wondering ... if your daddy didn't want to lose you and your mother, why did he let you go?"

"Let us go where?"

"Well, he didn't come with you. Did he say goodbye? How did you two get away when you came here?"

"Mama and I put some things in two pillowcases and walked out the front door. No one was at home. So we walked until we came to a gas station and found a man with a truck who was going to Indiana. Mama said we wanted to go to Fort Wayne and he said, 'Perfect. I'll call someone I know over there and he can find a place for us to rest when we get there.' Mama said she would just find her home and he could drop us off there. He said, 'Sure lady,' but I didn't like how he sounded. That's the sassy way Kevin Ledbetter would talk on the school playground when he was lying. But, Mama believed the man with the truck. When we got here, he wouldn't let us go."

"You said you left when everyone was gone? Where were they? Where was your dad? Did he kiss you goodbye?"

"He kissed me goodbye three days before that. I remember. They were all gone 'cause Grandpa wouldn't let us go." Tears again came to her eyes and filled them to the brim.

"Where wouldn't your grandfather let you go, Pooky?"

"To Daddy's funeral," she stopped for a moment and sobbed. When she rubbed her eyes on the full length of her shirt sleeve, she continued. "Daddy got really sick. Grandpa wouldn't let him go to the hospital, so he kissed me and Mama, "Goodbye," and died at our house." The salty tears streamed down her cheeks again. "He whispered in Mama's ear, 'Take Pooky and get out of here. Promise me.'"

"Mama said, 'I love you Steven. I promise.'" Pooky looked over at her mother where she and to her new grandparents stood crying. "Mama had never been out of the house before. At first it was so scary. We didn't know where to go. But, when Grandma and Grandpa left for the funeral, Mama and I walked right out the front door and didn't look back."

III

Backstory - 4

"This has just come into the news room," Clisty reported from the prompter as the eleven o'clock news program neared sign off. "Authorities tell WFT-TV that a woman came into police headquarters less than an hour ago. She said that a man had kidnapped her over eighteen years ago, just like the woman who was the hostage during the recent standoff between the accused bank robber and the police. For her safety, authorities are not releasing her real name. They are calling the woman, Darla." Clisty read calmly into the camera with the same confidence she had before she froze on TV when Faith first re-appeared.

"Darla told police that she managed to escape," Dan Drummond added to the report. "When the man stopped to use the restroom, before merging onto I-65 N, he forced her to stay in the truck. He told her she would never be able to get out. She said the doors weren't supposed to open from the inside. The only way you could get out was when the motor was still running. He would open the door, then turn off the engine and remove the key. She believed him—she wouldn't be able to get out of the truck because she had tried when he filled the gas tank closer to Fort Wayne. It was different at the intersection of I-65 N. This time he had failed to close his door all the way."

"That's right, Dan," Clisty tag-teamed the story. "She said she was able to get the driver's side door open, escape and jump, unseen, into the back of a truck going east. Luckily, the driver was going all the way back to Fort Wayne. She climbed out of the truck when the east bound driver stopped before entering the clover leaf at Goshen Road. The traffic was heavy as she walked along on the berm of the road. Then, she came upon a patrolman who, with his lights revolving, pulled a car over. She walked over to the officer, tugged his pocket and said, "I want to go home." At police headquarters, they quickly contacted her parents. With her mother and father present, she told her story to police."

"At the time of the attempted abduction, Darla was able to give the authorities a clue to the town in which the perpetrator probably lived. However, they were never able to find who had kidnapped her." Dan smiled and looked at Clisty.

He's giving me the last word. She smiled confidently and put on her professional, neutral, balanced face. "My investigation will include several threads of this tangled story: the background of the robbery suspect who was apprehended after the stand-off with police; the backstory of the hostage he held in the house; the details of an unsolved kidnapping nearly twenty years ago; and how the information of which Darla was able to remind police may answer questions to all facets of this story. All of these will be the focus of my expanded report in a new segment, *Stories from the Heartland.* I look forward to bringing you along as we follow the trail of clues to a hopeful resolution of this case. From the Fort, this has been News at Eleven."

"Great show people," Becca clapped her hands together as the network took over the feed.

Jake stood outside the studio window and watched. With his hands in his pockets, his tall slender frame exposed a leather cross-body gun holster. His eyes flashed brighter each time he looked at Clisty. "Ditto that," he agreed as soon as the studio door opened.

"Hi Detective," Clisty teased. "What brings you here so late in the evening?"

"You, of course," he spoke softly and stepped closer to her.

"Then, you are most welcome." Clisty slipped into the news room and started to pour a cup of coffee.

"Hold off on that last cup of the day," Jake warned. "I'm taking you out for decaf. It's late."

"Good idea," she agreed.

"But first, I brought in my Atlas. Come over here," he pointed to a table and spread out the book of maps.

"What's going on?" Becca asked as she joined them over the Rand McNally.

Jake was excited as he pointed to the map. "I read Darla's old file and found two details that add a lot to our quest." His index finger followed U.S. 30, north and west out of Fort Wayne. "She told police, her kidnapper said, 'only seventy more miles but first, I'm going to hit the head.' So ..." he traced the route that the man must have taken with his finger. "He was going to take route 65 north-west for seventy miles. He also said something about their destination being thirty miles west of Chicago." He targeted Chicago on the map, and then drew an imaginary line directly west of the city. "Wheaton, Illinois is ... twenty-eight mile west of Chicago ... Naperville is thirty miles." He thumped his finger on the spot between Wheaton and Naperville and drew a circle. "The place where Faith was held, is somewhere in this area." He grabbed Clisty in a side hug and didn't let go.

"The Freedom Temple," Becca hammered her fist into the palm of her hand. "If authorities in that area are aware of the Freedom Temple, maybe we can close in on the precise spot."

"Yes," Clisty snapped to attention from her cozy niche tucked under Jake's arms. "And, if we can find an elementary school that had a child named Pooky Jones for only two weeks, we will nail down the neighborhood."

"The last name she used, Jones, may be too general to track," Jake ran his hand over the back of his neck. "But, the first name, Pooky, sure isn't."

Clisty smiled. "It makes my hair stand up, too. It is so exciting."

"We are all tired, Honey," Jake said. "Let's start the computer search and telephone calls early tomorrow morning. It's not like Faith is still being held and we have to rescue her. It will do no one any good if we're too tired to think clearly."

"You're right; you're right; I know you're right, but—"

"No buts about it," Becca joined in. "I agree with Jake."

Clint had listened and watched as the three had inspected the map. A quiet guy, he turned and reached for his hoodie. "Just point me in the right direction, so I can aim the camera there. I'm going home and fall into bed." He zipped it up and started for the door. "I'll be here at the usual time, or whenever you tell me different. Just let me know if we're going to leave on a road trip so I can make arrangements for my cat. My wife has been visiting her mother."

"Bad Kitty?" Becca asked. "I don't know how you discipline that cat when you call, 'Bad Kitty' to give her a treat."

"She does seem a little neurotic at times," he admitted with a flippant expression. "Bye for now."

"Are you ready to surrender for the night?" Jake asked as Clisty continued to study the map.

"I guess," she drew out slowly. "I'm not sure I'll be able to sleep."

"Cocoa ... warm milk will help," he reminded her.

"I make cocoa with water," she corrected him and patted her stomach.

"I don't know what you have to worry about," Becca quipped. "You're so thin, I'm afraid to get a side view of you on camera. You might disappear altogether."

"Becca, don't be silly. You know as well as I do, if I were to gain ten pounds the station would replace me with a newer, slimmer model."

"Can't get much newer," Becca reminded her. "You're pretty young yourself. Beside, you know Fort Wayne viewers wouldn't put up with that. The station reflects the community's values of appreciation for hard work and family ties. You are family, Clisty."

"Thanks Becca. It's nice to be reminded."

"Then, ten pounds it is," Jake teased. "We'll stop at a grocery and pick up some milk. Made with water, it isn't cocoa at all. That's just chocolate flavored water." He took her by the elbow and started to steer her out of the news room. "Then, we'll go to your house and I'll make a cup for you." He stopped. "You do allow milk in your house, I hope."

"Fat free, of course."

"I'll think about that."

• • • • •

"But, Jake, whole milk? Isn't that a bit extreme?" Clisty complained as she took the milk and cocoa mix from the sack he had just carried into her apartment.

"Extreme will come when we put the whipped cream on the top," he said as he waved the squirt can in the air. He opened several cabinet doors until he found the measuring cups of various sizes. "Here we go."

"Do you really think we'll be able to find him and bring him to justice?" Clisty asked as she spooned some cocoa mix into the cups. Moments later, the microwave announced the hot milk.

"Find The Guardian?" Jake poured the steaming hot liquid into the cups, stirred in the cocoa and took them over to the coffee table ottoman. "Sure, I think we'll find him. But, I don't know when justice will be served."

"What does that mean?" Clisty followed him to the couch, folded her right leg under her and sat down on it.

99

"Justice usually takes time, Babe. Not your kind of time, as measured from one news headline at 6 p.m., to a verdict on the 11 o'clock news."

"I know. That's why I'm glad the network is giving me all the time that I need with the news magazine." She sipped the hot, bone warming, sleep inducing liquid and smiled. "This is good."

"Thank you," he said softly, stirred his cup again and drank a little of the sweet brew. There was tense silence for a moment until Jake asked, "When do you leave for New York?"

"I don't know," she sipped noisily. "I guess, the truth is, I don't really want to know." She reached over and took Jake's hand. "I just found Faith again and I know we're going to find her captors. But ... I also just found you."

Jake was quiet a while longer. "Have you talked to your grandmother about praying for you over this network business?" he asked and looked at the mantle. "That's your prayer angel, right?"

"No, I haven't called her yet ... I had to talk to you first," she sighed as her body reminded her of how tired she was.

"I appreciate that," he said as he smiled.

They finished their cocoa in silence, except for the soft music that streamed in the background. A deep baritone was spreading musical notes on the evening air like warm butter on toast. Jake reached over and traced gentle figure eights on Clisty's arm. Taking her cup, he placing it on the ottoman; then, he took her hand in his, all with the smooth gestures that matched the rise and fall of the melody.

"Faith just came home, Clisty, and that is wonderful. For me personally however, the real miracle is that I just found my home in you." Jake didn't stop. He continued, interrupting Clisty's effort to speak. "Now, don't misunderstand," he said softly. "I'm not saying— don't move to New York. That is an opportunity that very few people ever get. I wouldn't try to stop you for a minute. I'm just saying, with you in the east, will there be a place for me in your life?"

"Jake ... I am so torn," she began.

"Don't be, Honey. I'd never ask you to choose between New York City and me. That's not even a contest I want to enter. I guess I don't want to know who the winner would be." He caressed her hand, silently put his arm around her and drew her to his shoulder.

Clisty sat up quickly. "No, Jake, I admit I'm torn, but not between you and New York. The tug of war is between New York and Fort Wayne. See ..." she turned excitedly toward him and bubbled as she continued. "Since Faith came home; I'm seeing what really matters in my life. Yes, a job I love is important. But, the people I love, people Mom used to call my lovelies, are more valuable than anything else."

"I'm not sure if I fit in as a lovely," Jake laughed.

"You do, Jake Davis. You are the loveliest of lovelies," she laughed as she snuggled back under his arm.

"What I don't know," he admitted, "is how can you be in both places at the same time?" His eyes, cast down like a warrior who had just surrendered, didn't meet Clisty's.

"I can't Jake. But, that's all-or-none thinking. Just because I can't be in the TV studio and here in my apartment with you, does not mean there is no solution to this."

"That's good enough for me tonight," he said as he looked up with a sparkle in his eyes. He wrapped his arms around her, and surrounded her with his love.

"This is where I want to be, Jake—in your arms. I know that. Somehow, and I don't know how yet, I'm going to figure out how to do both. It's an old idea to think I can do everything. But, I can choose where I spend my time. I do know I'll have to do one thing at a time."

Part IV
The Quest - 1

The April sky greeted Clisty when she finally awakened the next morning. She stretched until the tiny kinks that stiffened her back gave up, let go and surrendered to her rhythmic twists.

"Good morning, day," she said as she shifted her feet off the bed and onto the floor. It would be an exciting day. She was confident that their research would find a clue that would lead them to The Guardian and his Lady, or the devil and his consort, which she thought was a much better description.

Even though she still wore her sleeping shorts and oversized t-shirt, she was compelled to get at her quest. A splash of water on her face and a tooth brush across her teeth, a habit she was unable to break no matter how much she wanted to skip it on busy mornings at home, and she was ready to open her laptop.

The familiar stream of coffee dripping into the pot on the kitchen counter was a welcome sound with an intoxicating aroma. The timer on the maker had been set the night before and now the fragrance was filling her apartment with a heavenly perfume. She used the seconds it took for her computer to boot-up to slip across the room and fill her cup. She was just putting it down on the end table beside the couch when her cell phone rang.

"Hello," she spoke into her smart phone, a little annoyed by the interruption—annoyed until she heard Jake's voice.

"Well, you're up earlier than I imagined."

"If you thought I was still asleep, why did you call?" she teased.

"I'm at your mercy, My Lady. I have no come-back for that logical question."

His voice was warm and creamy which prompted Clisty to remember the whole milk in the refrigerator. With her phone tucked under her chin, she took her cup back to the open kitchen and poured a little milk in her coffee.

"Have you been able to do any research on the location of the Freedom Temple?" she asked while stirring the creaminess into her java. She tried to make a fancy swirl on the top but decided that was a talent better left to coffee emporium artists.

"No, not I," Jake's voice dropped off with a sigh. "The Captain has me working on the bank robbery case. We want to make sure we can charge our man, Melvin Dean Fargo, with armed robbery in addition to kidnapping and Criminal Confinement. Rhodes is searching old files first. Then, he'll hit the computer."

"Okay, Jake. If I have a question I'll call the station and talk to Jeremy."

"Jeremy? Are you two on a first name basis now?" His voice was light and digging.

"Yes, Jeremy and I go way back ... almost a week now." She laughed and picked up her cup.

"It's not too early for your coffee, I hear by the sipping sound," Jake said. "I'm sitting here at my desk, doodling coffee cups on a post-a-note. Now, for some reason, I can't stop thinking of Faith's eyes, so sad, so empty and alone." He stopped. "Well, maybe not. She does seem to be stronger every time I see her." He paused, "How about ... I meet you for an early lunch, about 11:30? Maybe ... that new place we saw over near Jefferson Point Mall."

"That sounds wonderful." She placed her cup on the end table and smiled. There was a light layer of dust on the dark wood, not a lot, but … it was there. The more amazing point was … Clisty didn't care—not a whit. With the tip of her finger, she drew a happy face and laughed.

"You sound happy." Jake had a smile in his voice.

"I am." Her finger drew a curled mustache on her artistic dust-face. "I think I have just conquered an old fear," she shouted with glee, and turned her attention to the research. She ran her finger over the computer mouse pad and logged on. "I'll tell you what I find at lunch. See you there."

They said their goodbyes as Clisty turned to her glowing screen. First, she typed in the name, Melvin Dean Fargo. One site listed his age, fifty-seven; towns he had lived in, Fort Wayne, Indiana, Chicago, Illinois, and a couple of small towns in Tennessee; where he worked, where he studied and people to whom he was related.

"Chicago," she spoke into the empty apartment. "Okay, not west of Chicago, as Darla's driver/kidnapper had said."

"What about schools in Wheaton and Naperville," she continued to talk aloud as she changed her search input information along another line. She quickly came upon each of the elementary schools in the two towns, their addresses and phone numbers. She jotted down the names in Wheaton and contact information. Next, she typed in research parameters for elementary schools in Naperville. She identified each primary school and saved their "contact us" data. After writing it all down on a small note pad, she picked up her cell phone. She began a "rule out" search, by calling each school, in the order she had written the data.

Using a methodic research method, she wrote out a short script so she was sure to ask the same questions of each school.

1.   She would introduce herself and the TV station she represents.
2.   Her next question would be; was a student, by the name of Pooky Jones, enrolled there recently?
3.   Then, she would ask if the school had a mascot.

4.   Finally, she would find out if there is a church, named the Freedom Temple, anywhere in the area.

She got through the first two Wheaton schools with no success. Now, the phone was ringing at the third. She introduced herself and then asked her first question.

"I'm sorry, Ma'am. We do not give out the name of our students over the phone. If you want to bring in a written request, our principal may release that information since you said the child no longer attends here." The school secretary sounded sympathetic but could not bend the rules.

"Does the school have a mascot? Or, can you give me the mascot of the high school?"

"Wheaton North's mascot is the Falcon. Wheaton Warrenville South's mascot is the Tiger."

That doesn't line up, she thought. Then she asked, "Is there a church called the Freedom Temple in your area?" She held her breathe.

"I wouldn't call the Freedom Temple a church," the secretary drew out.

"So there is an organization called the Freedom Temple in Wheaton?" Clisty wondered if she had heard correctly.

"No, it's not here. A group by that name has been in the news from time to time."

"The news?" *Why didn't I research that so-called church first?*

"There have been newspaper and TV stories about several people, I think two women and a man, who told police they had wanted to leave the church and they were told they couldn't." The secretary talked in hushed tones, like someone would if they were sharing gossip.

"Do you know why they couldn't just ignore whoever told them they had to stay? What was their name, the person who told them they couldn't stop attending the church?"

"The Guardian. He's called, The Guardian. He manages to have all his followers sign over their home, their bank accounts, even their retirement investments to the Freedom Temple. If they quit attending the church, they forfeit everything."

"And, you said the Freedom Temple is there in Wheaton? Where exactly?" Clisty had her pen poised to write it all down.

"No, not here. It's someplace south of Wheaton. They are very secretive. They're out in the country on many acres, and back off the road." She spoke to someone in the office and then returned to the conversation. "That's really all I know and the principal needs me to look for a file. I hope that helps you," she said.

"That's a great help, thanks," Clisty touched the screen on her phone and ended the call. "That helps a lot," she talked to herself as she dialed the number of the first Naperville school. A computer generated map of that area of Illinois showed that Naperville lies in two counties. The northern part is in DuPage County, which allowed her to identify the northern edge of the school system and a probable school, positioned "south of Wheaton."

"Hello," a male voice at the school answered.

"This is Clisty Sinclair. I'm a news anchor with WFT-TV in Fort Wayne, Indiana."

"Good to talk to you, Miss Sinclair. I'm Roger Mitchel, the Principal here. What can I do for you?"

"I'm researching a story that appears to have a connection in your area. First, do you know if there is a church called, the Freedom Temple in your area?"

"Yes, there is a group ... no one knows much about them. Their church is off the road in a very remote, rural setting." Principal Mitchel also whispered into the telephone receiver. His muffled words sounded like he had cupped his hand around the mouth portion for privacy. "Their teachings are very different from those in our area. Their leader is both charismatic and controlling. As long as you obey his every command, including turning over all your money, property, everything, to The Guardian, you'll stay on his good side. If you refuse, he can get really mean. I'm sorry, but I think it's a cult."

"I have suspected the same thing," Clisty agreed. "I'm also asking the schools I contact what the school mascot is in their area."

"Mascot? Sure, we're Huskies up here," he said with pride.

"Big dogs," Clisty thought out loud.

"That's right. I guess we're all big dogs," he chuckled as he spoke.

"Now a question that may go beyond the bounds of confidentiality," she crossed her fingers as she asked. "I need to ask about a child who attended there for a really short period of time, for about two weeks. She was in a little school play, Little Red Riding Hood."

"Yes, the children did that play recently."

"Her name is Pooky Jones," Clisty reminded him.

"How could I forget a name like Pooky? I never heard that one before."

"I certainly have. That was my nickname when I was a child. Thank you so much. The TV crew and I will be in your area soon. May we stop by the school?"

"Certainly, I'd be happy to meet you. Please, make sure you don't video any of the children. That would breach their right to privacy–confidentiality rules and all."

"Certainly ... thank you Mr. Mitchel." They said their pleasant goodbyes and Clisty touched the *end call* on her phone. "That's it! Now, I have to talk to Jake!"

• • • • •

Clisty entered the café to meet Jake on the glorious April day. She looked around while her eyes adjusted to the dimer light inside.

Maneuvering past other diners, she slipped into a chair at his table. "You look good, Jake."

"I thought it was my job to say that to you," he said as he laughed. "You are enchanting."

"Well, you are supposed to say that I look good. And, I like *enchanting* even better. But, you, my laced up detective, live in the wrong century. Women can say how scrumptious their men look, too." She kissed him on the cheek, removed her jacket and placed it on the seat next to her.

"Their men? Your man?" His eyes shone.

"Yes, my man. Is that okay with you?" she narrowed her eyes like she was dodging a follow-up jab.

"Okay? It's far more than okay." He placed his hand on hers. "I'll admit I've been worried about you going to New York."

She started to open her mouth to speak, but he continued without yielding to the Gentle Woman from Fort Wayne. "I'm not saying I don't want you to succeed or have some fantastic opportunities. I'm saying ... I don't want to lose you."

Clisty put her hand on Jake's shoulder and leaned her chin on her hand. As a TV personality, she had a taboo about displays of affection out in the public. Actually, she was trying to hide the tears that had started to drown her. "I don't want to lose you either," she swallowed hard. "I guess I have been wondering if you will let me rise in my career, even help me to succeed."

"Let you? Don't ever think I might hold you back. I want to give you all the space you need," he choked on his words as his voice shook with emotion.

A waitress had walked past the table a few times until she finally interrupted softly. "Can I bring you two anything?"

"Coffee, black," Clisty responded quickly. "And, the pot too."

"Make that another cup and a really big pot," Jake added—his voice raspy with feelings.

Clisty rooted in her purse and pulled out a tissue that she dabbed under her lower eyelashes. She swallowed a little sip of water to flush out some emotional gravel from her throat. "I have some great news." She flashed a fresh smile and changed the subject.

"I am way overdue for good news," Jake said and patted Clisty's hand.

"I think I found the general location of the Freedom Temple—in Illinois, on the north side of Naperville. Pooky had attended school in that northern part of DuPage County for a few weeks and the principal remembered her." She sat back as the waitress placed two steaming cups of coffee in front of each of them. "Jake—we have him."

IV
The Quest - 2

"Do I have everything?" Clisty mumbled in the middle of her living room. "Maybe I'd better check it all again." Compulsively, she ticked off her list over and over, multiple times until she willed herself to stop. That didn't put an end to her anxiety however. "Maybe I'd better—" She stopped herself. "I'm ready. I have to let it go." She hung her head down, let her hands and arm swing freely, and let the blood rush to her head. She needed energy but not the kind of energy generated from nerves.

The next day was the day the quest was to begin. Clisty spent the evening staging her gear in the living room. She had finally put aside her fear of failure and put on success. Like an alter personality, her confident-self took over more frequently in recent days.

She had packed a zippered binder with all of her hand notes, laptop and iPad. She packed a travel bag with night shirt, make-up, a change of clothes and other toiletries. She was determined to take everything she needed and not stew about what she might have left behind. If they had to stay over, she would be ready.

Clisty heard an assigned cell ringtone. "Good Morning, Becca," she sang.

"I wanted you to know, I've made studio arrangements," she said excitedly. "I called North Central College's NCTV17 in Naperville. They have a link to Naperville Community Television. If necessary, you can broadcast from that remote location for the six o'clock news and the news at eleven." The tone of her voice bubbled. "It feels like this trip is falling into place."

"That's great, Becca! Your producer side is producing." She laughed and said, "I'm ready. I'll be there shortly."

Clisty lifted her jacket from the hall tree, gathered up her gear and carried it out to her parking space. She was excited as she loaded everything and hopped in her car that sunny morning and pointed it to the studio. So much had turned in the right direction. First, Faith was finally home. So far, she was just a reasonable facsimile of the Faith she would have been if she had grown up in Fort Wayne and gone on treasure hunts with Clisty. But, for now, Clisty would celebrate that she was home. Second, a new job came out of a dream she never knew she had. Her fantasy was to be a news anchor at a local station and balance that with a home, husband and children. Third, but certainly not the last of her blessings, there was Jake Davis. She pulled into the station parking lot just as her dream fully formed into the face of the police detective. "Hold that thought," she told herself. She hopped out of the car and hurried into the building.

"Jake Davis just called before you got here," Clint told Clisty as she walked into the newsroom.

"You said more in those eight words than I usually hear you speak in a week," she smiled as she slapped him on the shoulder.

"Then, I'd say ...," Clint paused and thought, "I'm done."

"Well, what did Jake have to say?" Clisty coaxed.

"Okay, these next words are for free, no charge. He said he'd be here in a few minutes. He was just leaving." Clint threw back his head and laughed. "You and Becca are the only people who think I don't talk much. My wife says I never shut up."

"This could be a long trip," Becca rolled her eyes at Clisty.

"Okay, it's about a hundred-and-sixty miles over there and should take us three and a half hours," Clisty calculated. "It's ... eight fifteen. If Jake gets here in the next fifteen minutes, we should get to Naperville about noon. The school should be nearing the end of their lunch schedule by then."

"No, the beginning of the rotation," Jake said from behind her.

Clisty jumped. "You startled me," she moaned with a smile on her face. She was glad Jake was back to his joking self.

"I heard what you were saying when I came in," Jake joined in. "Illinois is on Central time, so we'll get there around eleven o'clock, our twelve, just as they start their lunch cycle." He held up a dark brown duffle. "I have my go-bag in case we need to stay over. No one's waiting for me. Are you all ready to go?"

"I think we are, complete with travel bag and two pair of shoes, walking and sitting." Clisty patted the colorful print on her duffle. "I was thinking," she admitted as she hoisted her bag to her shoulder, "all of our plans may change, depending on what we find. We may have to leave Naperville in a hurry."

"Is that a premonition?" Becca asked with measured gaze.

"No ... logic. So far, everyone, including my memory as a child, has reported that The Guardian is a very mean and dangerous man." Her eyes narrowed. "We may have to cut our trip short. We might even have to go back some other time to finish our investigation. For now, let's agree to error on the side of caution."

"I agree one-hundred percent," Jake said and the others added a firm. "Yes."

The four gathered all their personal baggage and the station gear and took it all out to the van. Becca helped Clint load the camera and other equipment.

"I'll drive, Clint, so you can get some shots out the window when we get near Chicago." Becca put the station van keys in the ignition.

"Sure," Clint nodded. "That makes sense. Besides, you usually don't relinquish your control on—"

"Are you saying I'm controlling," she snapped?

"I'm saying I'll be happy to film the trip," he said and settled back into his usual elective mute self. He hopped up into the co-piolet's seat; that left Clisty and Jake in the back.

"Have you planned a route?" Becca pulled to the edge of the parking lot and waited for driving instructions.

"We'll take US 30 northwest out of Fort Wayne," Clisty thought out loud. "I think that may have been the way they went." She checked the map again. "Darla said she escaped when her kidnapper got out of the truck before he merged onto I-65, off US 30."

"I wish I could fluff my pillow and curl into a kitten ball," Becca sighed. "But, some people say drivers can't do that."

In the back seat, there was an uncomfortable silence. Clisty watched the scenes pass by outside her window but nothing caught her eye. Jake was silently surveying the view on the right. The longer they sat motionless, the louder the silence between them became.

"I don't know what to say," she whispered.

"About what?" Jake questioned from his side of the car, actually a mile away in emotional measurement.

"I guess I was thinking out loud ... never mind." She didn't look at Jake, although it felt like he had fixed his eyes on her, even though she knew he had turned his head away.

The energy between them was alive with magnetism. There was a force that neither could deny. Jake reached over and took Clisty's hand. She wanted to fold herself into his arms and lay her head on his shoulder, but her own professionalism didn't permit back seat cuddling. She stole a look at him and his eyes were so full of raw feelings, she blushed. There were things to say, but that was neither the time nor the place.

· · · · ·

They followed Route 30 West for one-hundred seventeen miles, and then connected to I-65 and drove north to Gary. It would have been a shorter route to by-pass Chicago and go directly to Naperville, but, they weren't on a family outing. They had video to take to accompany the story of Faith's journey to freedom.

Gary, Indiana appeared as busy and frantic as usual from the highway that rose up above the chaos. "I know we are taking the long way," Clisty said as she watched the route out the windshield and the side windows. "But, we want Clint to get some good video of Chicago." In Gary they took I-80/90 toward Chicago.

Becca pointed to a sign down the highway. "Look, at the next exit there's a Starbucks. Let's stop there, get something to drink, and Clint can film us and the area." As she neared the exit, they all straightened up, stretched and cleared their eyes. "I'll pick something up for you while you film, Clint. What do you want?"

"Straight up coffee, black," he said as he unpacked his equipment in preparation for filming. He had stowed the shoulder-held camera bag beside him in the van.

When they stopped, Jake jumped out, came around the van and took Clisty's hand as she stepped out onto the ground, freshly washed by a light spring rain. "Are you tired?" he asked.

"Thank you kind Sir," she remarked about the gallantry. Then she denied, "No, I'm too excited to be tired. Besides, if I admitted it, I'm afraid I'd fall over where I stand." She wiggled and twisted as she walked to the door, hoping to fully wake up.

Inside the store, Clisty bought her usual, café mocha. "I'm out of my element," she said as she sipped a little of the whipped cream off the top. "It feels safer to stick with what I know."

"And you're considering a move to New York City?" Becca's eyes popped. "Illinois makes you uncomfortable and you're debating the merits of moving to New York?"

"I know," Clisty sighed, "I hear ya. I don't want to think about that adjustment right now, but ... I hear ya."

Jake smiled, rolled his eyes and ordered a vanilla cream steamer, made with half-and-half and plenty of whipped cream on the top. Since ten pounds wouldn't even appear on his slim frame, he ordered a venti. They took their cups and went back to the van.

"Okay, Clint" Becca said as she placed her coffee in the cup holder. "If you took enough video of this area, we'll press on. We'll be passing by Chicago in a little while. Have your camera ready."

As they drank their coffee and moved along toward Chicago, Clint filmed some of the tall buildings of the city before they turned west on I-88. "I got some good stuff," Clint said.

At I-88 they dropped south on Route 34. "Good," Clisty said as she checked the map, "this places us on the north side of Naperville."

They traveled over two-hundred miles, due to their detour into the Chicago area, which brought them to the circular driveway of Principal Mitchel's elementary school around noon, Indiana time. Becca parked in a student-pickup spot and hopped out. Clint got out and positioned the camera, while Clisty jumped from the van and took a reporters position in front of the double school doors.

Clisty pointed to the sign with the school name over the door. "Make sure that the school name is not in focus and there are no children in the background. We simply cannot invade their privacy. Besides, identifying the school doesn't advance the story in any way. These people have only been helpful."

"Okay, Clint, send a link to my tablet so I can see your lens view," Becca said as she touched the screen on her iPad. Quickly the scene in front of the school popped up on her tablet. "I can still see the school name, Clint. Pan down a little." She studied the screen. "Good, hold it there."

A man with a closely clipped graying beard walked out of the school and approached the crew. "I saw the name of your station on the side of your van," he said as he reached out his hand to Clisty.

"You must be Principal Mitchel, Sir," she greeted him. "I'm Clisty Sinclair."

"Mr. Mitchel," Becca reached out and shook his hand, "I'm Rebecca Landers, producer-director of the six and eleven o 'clock WFT news." She stepped beside him and offered to share her e-tablet. "I can show you the angle we are taking." She offered him an opportunity to peruse the view finder.

"Oh, that looks fine," Mitchel said. "That could be any elementary school in Illinois. When the children go out for recess, they will go out the back doors. All play areas are behind the school."

"Mr. Mitchel, have you found any other information about Pooky Jones?" Jake asked and extended his hand. "I'm Jake Davis, a Fort Wayne police detective."

"Detective, I'm glad to meet you." He raked his fingers through his hair. "I've been thinking about Pooky Jones and the Freedom Temple since you called. May I ask what all of this is about?"

"We can tell you what the Fort Wayne viewers have already been told. First, the bank robbery," Clisty nodded at Jake to let him answer the police questions.

When Jake and the WFT crew brought Principal Mitchel up to date, he was silent. "Right here in our own town ... and no one knew."

"Don't blame yourself, Sir. I've blamed myself for many years. The Guardian kidnapped Pooky's mother right out of my living room when we were both nine years old. He jerked her out of my hand, and all I could do was run and hide." Clisty cleared her throat and regained her composure. "I've learned that evil gets its way sometimes, but when good people can put a stop to it, they do."

"I've noticed you have had the camera rolling for a while." The principal was thoughtful for a moment. "You don't need to use my name. The story isn't about me or this school. It has taught me that we have to be on watch for all of our children. In the building in which I did my student teaching, the teachers made a home visit to each of their student's homes. I have tried to do that here. When the teacher called to set up a time to make a home visit, the parents of the child in question immediately pulled her out of school. I will instruct my teachers to report any similar incidents that may happen. Social services or a school psychologist should follow up with a home visit of their own. We have to assume the parents had something to hide, until an inquiry proves another cause for withdrawing the child."

"Can the school psychologist do that, if a child is no longer enrolled?" Jake asked with legal issues in mind.

"That's a good question. We'll check with our legal department. I know CPS can make a contact. For the school, at a minimum, a teacher could offer information about home schooling guidelines and perhaps, a list of programs a home-schooled child can participate in, within the public school system. Whether the child is in the school community or not, they could still be part of the educational outreach of the school."

"So, as a principal, you're not against home schooling?" Clisty asked, and then pointed the microphone back to Mitchel.

"There are many reasons why home schooling is a better option for a particular child. The neighborhood can still offer group sports, band and choir participation, and many other in-school and out-of-school activities. Classes with science labs also come to mind."

"Thank you, Sir," Clisty said then turned to the camera. "That is the first in our kaleidoscope of vignettes that will tell the story from the heartland about a child who was lost and has now been found."

Once the camera was off, Clisty asked, "Can you tell us where the Freedom Temple is or a good guess as to its location?"

Principal Mitchel brightened, "I am honored to tell you what I know. It sounds like The Guardian is not a protector of children." He stroked his beard. "There is a plot of land out in the country all of us have wondered about. There are quite a few acres and it sits off the road. The buildings aren't as visible from the road when the trees are full; but you should be able to see it now. It has a fence around it."

"Can you give us directions?" Jake asked.

"Go down about five miles, turn left on Old Mill Road and follow it ... here, let me jot it down." Principal Mitchel took a business card from his pocket and sketched out the location. "There you are," he said as he handed it to Clisty. "Now, I have to get back in, so my secretary can go to lunch."

"Thank you so much," she said and waved.

After the principal went back inside, Clisty's was unable to pass as Jake stepped into her space. She looked toward the school and whispered to Jake without looking at him. "There are a lot of kids watching us Jake. We're the big TV stars, I guess; although, I feel like Grandma's Pooky who needs a hug."

"I'll be happy to provide the arms," he said with a smile.

"Don't forget that offer," she said as she waved at the excited, curious children at the school windows.

"I plan to always have ready arms," he whispered low enough Becca and Clint wouldn't hear.

Clisty took him by the hand and walked around to the other side of the van. She checked the school for visibility then threw herself into his arms. He didn't withhold a single unit of kinetic energy. Clisty received his love and covered his face in kisses.

"Does this mean that you have changed your mind about the network's offer?" Jake's voice was raspy with the strength of his passion for her.

She pulled back and studied his face. "No. I haven't decided. But, are you saying you won't accept my love ... unless I turn the network down?"

"Are you two ready?" Becca asked as she got into the van.

"Yes," Clisty snapped as she pulled away from him.

"No, we're not," Jake insisted and took her arm.

"Jake, don't," she sighed.

"Honey ... okay," he threw up his hands in surrender. "Just know, I did not say that at all, because that's not what I meant."

She stopped and placed her hand softly over Jake's heart but could not meet his eyes. She didn't move on but stood there for a moment.

Jake put his hand on top of hers and caressed her fingers. "Can we at least say this conversation isn't over?" Jake asked.

"You bet your shinny badge it's not over," she said, looked into his eyes and felt his fire.

IV

The Quest - 3

"Becca, everything is stowed." Clisty said as she slapped the back door of the closed van. She slid into the second row of seats beside Jake.

"I am so ready for this, I can't catch my breath." Clisty rubbed her hands together, like she was ready to tackle a two-hundred-fifty pound football player. "Do you know how long I have wanted to get that guy who took Faith?" She stopped and thought. "I know, eighteen years. But, for me it seems like a lifetime."

"It has been," Jake fastened his seatbelt and sat back. "It's been your whole adult life. You finally got to the age that you felt strong enough to confront your nightmares."

"Jake, how did you know?" Clisty was amazed.

"When kids have been traumatized and made to feel they are helpless to do anything about it, they say, 'I'm a weak and awful person.' Or, they say, 'No, the offender is wrong and will be punished.' They bring their monster to justice, within what their moral fiber tells them, and their mental health tempers their revenge."

As the motor hummed, Clint slowly pulled the van out of the school drive. Jake reached out, took Clisty's hand and squeezed it. Clisty smiled, watched the world out of her side window, and then gently squeezed his hand back.

Jake pulled his cell phone from his pocket and texted, "Does your hand say we're still talking?"

She felt her cell vibrate, fished in her pocket and smiled as Jake's name appeared on her screen. She texted, "Yes—we're still talking. I just talked to you."

"Is there a problem?" Becca asked from the co-pilot seat.

"No, we ..." Clisty stopped when she saw Becca smile and glance down at Clisty's phone. "No, no problem. Mom texted a question about the trip."

"Your mom? Texted you?" Her smile took on an impish expression.

"Why don't you take a nap, Becca?" Clisty shooed her hand and dismissed her friend from the conversation. "It's five miles to our first turn."

While Becca turned around and snuggled into her pillow, Clisty ran her fingers over the touch pad. "Is the NY job a deal breaker?" she texted.

"Job? No." Jake texted. "NY not a prob."

"Then, what?"

"Hon, it's the distance that's the prob," his fingers entered into the text message.

Clisty put her phone in her pocket, grabbed Jake's arm and pulled him to her so she could whisper in his ear. Cupping her hand, she said, "As long as I don't have to choose between us and the job, we'll figure out the rest of it." She caressed his cheek and lingered there, close, like someone warming themselves by a fire.

Clint said nothing as he drove. To Clisty, Clint seemed relaxed, but suddenly, his hands tightened on the steering wheel and he pulled himself up straight, to military attention. "Five miles—this is our first turn," he announced. Everyone in the car tensed.

Clisty tried to prepare herself mentally. They were going to try to get in the Freedom Temple, a place so secret, no one seemed to know exactly where it was. "It's broad daylight," she thought out loud. "We can't sneak through an open door. They would see us approach."

Clint pulled over. "Don't you find it a little strange that we hadn't thought this through first? The TV camera and van have WFT-TV on it. They might easily put Fort Wayne with WFT."

"Especially if The Guardian has been to Fort Wayne before," Jake added.

"Well," Clisty snapped, "I know he has."

Clint drove several more miles, turned south, then west. "Have a look at that." His voice dripped with awe.

Out in front, a high, wrought iron fence stretched along the left side of the road. Since it was April, the trees weren't in foliage; they could see a massive structure in the center of an English style garden of hedges and flower beds, barely awakening from the winter.

"Amazing!" Clisty slowly found words to express what the other stunned crew did not say. "There's no sign, no boastful declaration that you have arrived at the Freedom Temple. But, this has to be it. What else could it be out here?"

"Will you look at that?" Jake pointed to the gate while everyone else focused on the house. He started to open the van door.

"Where are you going?" Clisty asked.

"The gate ... look ... it's not locked." He jumped out and pushed the tall, heavy black decorative iron open. It swung heavily, like an entrance to a deceptively beautiful, yet evil mansion in a horror movie. Clint pulled slowly through the opening and stopped to pick up Jake on the other side.

A densely wooded area stood on the right of the acreage and also the far left. In the center of the compound, down a slight hill, a castle style building rose up from the basement, to what appeared to be an attic or second story with four dormers. A wide porch stretched across the full expanse of the front of the building. Cement steps, that resembled those of a county courthouse, gave a false message of welcome. There was no welcoming vibration coming from the place at all.

"We're in; now what?" Becca's voice shook with excitement.

"Why isn't anyone around?" Clisty asked; her eyes vigilant. Lights were visible through sheer curtains at windows to the right, the only clue that there might be people inside. Three cars sat alone in the V.I.P. marked parking spaces. The rest of the massive lot was empty.

Becca placed her hand on the dashboard and looked as far in every direction as she could twist. "I thought this was a secure compound. I don't see guards or even people outside enjoying the day."

Jake searched the surroundings with a detective's eye. "Will you look at that," he whispered. "That front door isn't closed either," he searched with intent surveillance. "Be very careful, everyone. There's something very strange here."

Everyone in the car adopted a stealth mode. Ducked heads and whispered voices plotted out their next move.

"Before we pull up to the door," Becca said as she started setting up camera angles, "Clint, you hop out and start filming the building and area. I want the woods, the empty parking pad over there, the front door partially open, and finally, the three of us planning our strategy."

"Got ya," Clint shouldered the TV camera and spanned the full scope of the compound. The sky was blue and provided a counter-emotional backdrop for the scene. "Dark clouds or lightning bolts would make a more accurate depiction for the shot," he protested. "I guess it does show how deceptive it is."

Clisty itched to have her first look inside. "Let us know when you have what you want, Clint. Then, Becca, let's all get out and approach on foot."

"The elevation slopes slightly," Jake pointed to the terrain. "Once Clint has the camera shots he needs, Clisty and I will get out here. Becca you get behind the wheel and allow the van to coast as far as it will move. Our escape vehicle will be closer if we have to make a quick exit."

"I like that idea," Clint agreed as he leaned into the van window. "I have some great footage. You can move."

Clisty and Jake got out. Those on foot waited while Clint positioned the camera again and took some shots of the wooded surroundings and then panned to images of Clisty, Jake and the moving van.

Clisty looked at the mansion and shook her head. With its open door, it looked like a surprised giant with a gapping mouth. Becca put the van in gear and coasted toward the building. Clint attached a microphone to the camera and checked the connection.

Not knowing how hostile those inside might be, Clisty and Jake walked behind the van, using it as a shield until it stopped rolling. Once Becca was as near to the Temple as she could get, she put the van in park, stowed the keys in her zippered side pocket, and followed the others as they approached the front door on foot. Up the steps, tread by tread, like a conquering army, they cautiously entered, with camera aimed. They slipped through the door and assessed the interior.

The floor was glowing white marble. Light coming through the windows, danced off the recrystallized calcite, and sparkled beneath their feet. White columns rose from the floor to the second story balcony above. Through tall, heavy open doors to the left they could see a huge gathering room. Clisty took mental notes of everything she saw. One might call the room a large sanctuary, if there were anything holy about the place.

Jake put his index finger to his lips and pointed to the right. Angry, muffled voices came from a room with the door ajar. Clint aimed the camera and its microphone toward the door.

"What happened, Guardian?" one angry, frightened voice demanded. "They are all gone, even my woman. She took my son."

His words spit out like rounds from a Gatling gun, fast and furious. "My son!"

"Where's Emily?" another voice demanded.

"Don't you ask about my Lady, Mister." A third voice ordered. "She's at our home where she belongs. She hadn't asked to go anywhere this morning, so she's there." His words were those of authority. "I've trained her proper!"

"That doesn't tell me what happened!" the first one shouted.

"It's Jocelyn," The Guardian accused. "She escaped when we were at Steven's funeral. She took the kid, too."

"Jocelyn, who is Jocelyn?" one of the men questioned.

Clisty cringed. She knew full well who Jocelyn was. Now, The Guardian was blaming Faith for whatever happened to jeopardize his control over the people of the Temple. The fear she felt for Faith's safety had grown to near panic. People with so much power, based on some twisted self-created religious conviction, were not only irrational, they were extremely dangerous.

The other one threw in a hostile accusation. "What happen to your clan, Guardian? Don't they obey you anymore?" The anger in his voice frightened Clisty. She knew how volatile people can be when someone challenges their delusions. Her heart pounded wildly. Those inside the adjacent room could erupt into a violent brawl at any time, or even a battle if they were armed.

"Jocelyn is his daughter," one said with disgust.

"Your daughter?" the other questioned. The pitch of his voice approached rage. "Why has she never been at the Temple? Why have we never seen her?"

"She's been rebellious since we adopted her," The Guardian stated with anger, but with less conviction.

"Tell him about Pooky," the first one insisted with venom in his words.

"What's a Pooky?"

"Pooky is a who, not a what." The Guardian explained.

The volume in the accuser's voice rose again. "Go ahead," he shouted, "tell him about Pooky."

"Shut your mouth," The Guardian demanded, but his voice had lost its edge of authority. "Pooky is my granddaughter, Steven's son."

"What!" One of them roared? "Where have they been ... locked up in your house? Have you held them captive? What if someone saw them?" The questions fired like an assassin's bullets.

"We'd all be at risk," the other one gasped.

"No one knows where I live," The Guardian insisted. "We live on a quiet, shady street like any respectable neighbor. I have been very careful."

"Are you crazy, or what?" One asked accusingly, his voice cracked with anger. "Everyone knows where the 'scary man in the black house' lives!"

Clisty's eyes snapped to Jake's. He gave a wind-up gesture with his finger in the air, and all four of them silently backed out of the house. They had a lead, enough to continue the search in town. Now, they had to move. Clisty was giddy with excitement and nearly overwhelmed with fear.

Without a word, they all tiptoed back to the door, down the front steps and out to the van. Jake got in behind the wheel and Clisty took the co-piolet seat. Becca pulled the key out of her pocket and handed it to Jake from the middle row. When he put the key in the ignition, the engine seemed to roar, but he had to start it. There was no way to coast up hill. A fast escape or a slow one would create the same noise once the van started and speed was their only means of success. They all slammed their doors closed in union while Jake made a one-eighty in the wide drive. Inside the van there was breathless silence however, until they passed the open gate at the entrance. The danger was too great to talk about it until they were on the road again.

"We're all safe," Jake reminded them. "Now breathe slowly and your heart will stop racing."

Clisty thought of the prayer angel on her mantle. She had prayed for Faith and her own grandmother had prayed for her. Peace settled in like sunshine brings joy on a rainy day. She was ready for the next step in their quest. "A single black house on a Naperville street," Clisty finally announced with determination. "Lady, here we come."

"I hope we're the only ones heading to that house," Becca announced as she turned and searched the empty road behind them through the rear window. "They're not back there yet, but they certainly heard us when we left. There was no way to move the vehicle without starting the motor. They may follow and they'll get there first since they know where they're going."

"Then we have to get there fast." Jake said.

"Are you armed?" Clint asked.

"Of course," he said and patted the right side of his jacket.

"I hope it doesn't come to that," Clisty whispered. "We came to rescue the lady, not get her executed."

IV

The Quest - 4

Naperville lay in front of them, a sprawling extension of Chicago along the Burlington North Santa Fe Metro line, just thirty miles west of the city. Clisty could easily see it was no longer the sleepy college town her grandmother had told her about when she met her grandfather there as a college freshman. As she watched the city stretch out its new streets, she wondered what it was like back when her grandparents knew it. Now, red brick sidewalks and streets were enchanting, like something out of an old movie she had seen on TV. Quaint old buildings with overhanging bay windows blended with new stores like Barnes and Noble Booksellers and a fancy Pizzeria with a festive red awning for dining on the sidewalk. She took out her e-tablet and cleared her head by typing in the mental notes she had taken earlier. There was no time for reminiscence.

"Who knows something about Naperville?" Jake asked as he slowly wound through the city streets.

"Nothing really," Clisty said as she watched for directional clues she knew would not appear. "Faith never left the house and Pooky was outside for only two weeks."

"We're wasting a lot of time wandering around. We might not get back to Indiana by the six p.m. news," Becca reminded them. "I called North Central College on my cell and took them up on their offer to let us use their studio. If we shoot a segment there, they can send it on to WFT, and the station will air it when the six o'clock news hour comes around."

"Well, okay, maybe," Clisty grinned broadly. "But they'll have to take me without professional makeup on."

"You are beautiful all the time," Jake patted her knee.

"I have a little blush in my purse and I'm sure you have lipstick," Becca offered.

"Where is the college, Becca?" Jake asked.

"Well, it's one-hundred-fifty years old … so it would be in the original part of town," she offered as she continued to watch out the window. "They gave me the address and I wrote it all down," she watched the passing street signs. "Here … turn here, Clint. This street sounds right. Let's hurry. We don't have much time."

They stopped in front of the building that housed the television station and all four hurried from the van. Clisty buttoned her jacket as the April breeze caught it and blew it opened. Hurrying in, Becca led the way and introduced the entourage to the station manager who was waiting for them.

"I'm so happy you could help us today," Clisty said as she followed the man into the studio. She whipped out her lipstick and swished the brush to Becca's blush across her cheeks.

As they approached the door to the studio, the phone on the station manager's desk rang. "Yes?" he asked into the receiver. "Oh, no." Then he placed his hand over the phone and spoke to Becca. "I am so sorry. There is a huge breaking story that will have to take your spot in the studio." He listened again and then spoke into the phone, "Okay, we'll send a crew out immediately."

"What happened?" Clisty asked.

"There is a cult on the north side of the county, the Freedom Temple. Someone is actively setting fires out there. According to witnesses who happened upon the compound, new fires continue to ignite. They're in various parts of the temple and out-buildings."

Clisty looked from Jake to Becca. "The Freedom Temple is burning. The Guardian's Lady could be in danger. We have to get to her right away."

All four of them put their jackets back on and started for the door. Becca turned to the manager, "Thank you so much for your generous offer. We certainly know how quickly the news changes. The fire at the Freedom Temple may have put someone else at risk. We'll have to get to her fast. Please, feed the video you have of the fire to our studios in Fort Wayne. We'll share our information about Naperville's connection to Fort Wayne when we have it compiled. Okay?"

"Absolutely," the manager said as he shifted into *breaking-story mode* and notified his people just as Clisty and the group went out the door.

"Okay, people," Jake announced. "Now where?"

"Pooky said she watched children as they walked home from school. If that's the case, we've gone too far into Naperville," Clisty began to realize. "We need to be on that north side again." Clisty touched her cell phone screen and brought up a map of the north side. "We got detoured by our concern over the early newscast."

"That's right," Becca agreed. "The house can't be too far from the school. Finding the Freedom Temple out in the country led us away from the residential areas."

"Somehow, I thought the house would be an old Victorian because of the size," Clisty felt energized by getting back to the facts of the case. "But, it wouldn't have to be."

"That Temple is a mansion. Why can't The Guardian's house be a large, new home in one of the northern suburbs?" Becca jumped into the excitement of the hunt.

Clisty searched the passing streets for a clue to the location. "It's hiding in plain sight."

• • • • •

Jake coasted the van up and down neighborhoods on the north side of town. They trolled from street to street and subdivision to subdivision. "I hope no one reports us for stalking," Jake cracked.

Clint offered a plausible excuse. "You can call it surveillance."

"I could if I carried a Naperville Police badge," Jake said and then slowed to a stop. "Look up there in the next block."

"Where?" Becca reached for the back of the front bucket seat and searched the block ahead of them.

"Right there," Clisty whispered. Her voice caught in her throat. She wasn't sure if she was the hunter or the hunted. She had the persona of a victim hidden in the secret corner of her mind. Most of the time she had been able to keep it locked away from view. Faith's return, the presence of the bank robber, and the voices of the men at the Freedom Temple were too much for the guards at the gate of her secret thoughts to keep her fears at bay.

Ahead and to the right, a mammoth black stone edifice rose up out of the ground like an ancient giant, imposing and menacing. The windows had some sort of opaque coating that glowed black in the high day sun. Window wells beneath the foundation revealed the obvious presence of a basement. "Complete with dungeon," Clisty gasped.

"First and second floors, plus an attic," Jake ticked off the enormity of it. "I'm surprised it sits as close to the sidewalk as it does. Mansions usually hide from traffic, back long paved driveways. This one would invite visitors, if it weren't so scary."

"Jake, look," Clisty pointed. "Along the front fence at the end of the sidewalk, there's a rock garden, all polished and sparkling. Pooky said, 'She would leave a note for me under a rock near the end of our sidewalk.' Jake, she gave us a clue she wasn't aware she had." Then Clisty began to remember something else as she pulled another fragment from what Pooky had said. "Leenie Lambert, 1221 W. Benton Avenue."

"The cross street we just passed was W. Benton," Jake said with a thumb pointing back over his shoulder.

"What?" Becca asked. "Benton and the rocks?"

"The rocks at the end of the sidewalk. I have to investigate." Clisty turned and looked through the back window. "The coast is still clear. We'd better hurry though. The Guardian can come at any time. He's burning all bridges behind him. His Lady may be his beloved wife, but my guess is, she's totally expendable."

"The Guardian could get here as quickly as he set those fires. He may not even know that we found him there. But, he seems to believe his cult-kingdom has been threatened with exposure and he's blaming his home situation," Jake warned.

"Clint, you get out and take your initial shots of the house from up the street at our present location. Use the zoom lens in case there's a chance of finding someone in an open window or at the door," Becca started setting camera angles immediately.

Clint got out and shouldered the camera. "The street is clear," he observed. "You guys get closer and I'll start shooting from here. I'll be able to capture your approach to the house."

Jake rolled slowly toward the house, watching in every direction, windshield, back and both side windows. He parked in front, where a short wrought iron fence identified the property line. At the corner, the rocks piled on both sides, inside and outside of the marked off area. "I know we look obvious from inside. Even the neighbors can read our station number and logo plastered on the side of the van. We can't help it. If we have to run to the van, some of us may not be able to keep up."

"Hey, Detective Skinny," Becca corrected, "I can run just as fast as the rest of you. I've been working out, ya know."

"I'll jump out and check the rocks." Clisty had the door open before anyone could respond. She quickly looked up and down the rock garden that sparkled with an occasional quartz stone. Bending down, she hurriedly lifted a three inch round stone and slowly pulled a small piece of paper from beneath it, careful to touch only the extreme corners.

Becca and Jake had gotten out and had gathered around her. "What does it say?" they asked in unison.

"Where are you Pooky?" Clisty read. "Are you OK?" She handed the paper to Jake. "For the evidence bag."

Jake pulled a small zip lock plastic bag from his shirt pocket and held it out for Clisty to drop the paper in. "Good start," he said but kept looking out the back for any signs of danger. "Keep your eyes open."

As Clisty watched Jake zip the bag closed, she thought about Leenie Lambert, who had wondered where Pooky had gone, just as she always wondered where the kidnapper had taken Faith. "I don't think I'll close my eyes again until this whole case is solved," she pronounced.

"Now what?" Clint asked as he walked up beside them as they stood by the rock garden.

"Put the camera in the van and take the segment inside the house, if we can get in, on your smaller one." Clisty suggested. "You're a great cinematographer. You would be able to get great video with a child's toy camera."

"Amen to that," Becca agreed. "We can't waste any more time. The neighbors will start wondering what a TV crew is doing on their safe, quiet street. Soon, the Lady inside will see us and might even call her husband. She doesn't know that things have changed."

"Okay, let's do this." Clisty squared her shoulders, "We aren't going to doubt ourselves, or be nervous about anything. We're the news and we're getting our story. We're going right up to the front door," Clisty stated with determination.

They all approached the home in silence as they surveyed the house with the heavy eight foot front door. Clisty took the lead and lifted the brass knocker. Each looked at the other as they waited with rehearsed calm, trying hard to control their impatience.

"Yes?" a tired looking, middle-aged woman said when she opened the door a few inches.

"Good afternoon," Clisty began slowly as she thought fast. "Is Joselyn home?"

The woman's eyes grew large as she closed the door to a crack. "How do you know Joselyn?"

"We talked one day ... in the back yard ...," Clisty stammered as she tried to find an answer that would sound plausible to the woman. "Ah ... I'm Clisty Sinclair. We talked about my daughter, Leenie. She wants to find a time to play with Pooky."

"Pooky?" the woman asked and opened the door a little more.

"I'm in a bit of a hurry. My friend and I would love to come in your lovely home. I ... ah work for a TV station and we've considered a show in which we would tour beautiful homes in the Midwest. Perhaps you would allow the cameras in here. May we come in? I'd like to take a few notes, in case you think you might be interested in the near future."

"Well, I don't know," she hesitated but slowly stood back and let them in. "I am very proud of our home. But, I don't know what my husband will say." The entry and grand staircase in front of them had flooring and treads of the same marble that graced the floor of the Temple. A crystal chandelier hung suspended over the foyer from the ceiling and reached the full height of the two stories. Clisty marveled at the polish and shine on every surface, free from dust and smudges.

"Come into the parlor," the woman said. "You're not going to film anything now are you? I'll have to ask my husband first."

"Clint left the big TV camera in the van," Becca told her. "He does have a very small one with him and he'll probably get a few shots."

Lady, as Faith had called her, directed them to the large, thickly carpeted room to the right of the entry hall. "Please take a seat," she offered as she sunk heavily into an overstuffed chair beside the fireplace.

"I'm Clisty Sinclair," she introduced herself again, "and this is my producer and director, Rebecca Landers. Clint usually handles the camera, and this is my friend Jake Davis. I'm sorry, Ma'am," Clisty began as she sat on the sofa. "I have forgotten your name."

"Emily Treadway. That's okay, I forget a lot, too."

"You and Dave have lived here ... "Clisty laid out a prompt for the next answer.

"No, Ezra," she corrected. "Not Dave."

"Oh, my goodness, I forgot again." She apologized. "Of course ... Ezra. Is he home? I haven't met him yet."

Emily's eyes darted back and forth, frightened, tense. "No, he's not here. You can't meet him."

"That's okay," Clisty quickly answered and smiled calmly, hoping Emily would catch a little of the peace for herself. "We first stopped at the Temple," she began cautiously, with no seeming concern.

"You got inside the Temple?" the woman questioned. "How is that possible?"

"Everything seemed fine to us," she turned to the others. "Didn't it? Calm, mostly quiet."

"Oh yes," Jake said casually. "The front gate was open and welcomed us. The front door, too."

Clisty continued as if there was no cause for worry or fear at all. "No one seemed to be around though. At first we thought the place was empty."

"Empty?" Emily asked again.

"Then, we heard a man talking, two others referred to him as The Guardian. They sounded really angry. We didn't stay long enough to hear all of what they were yelling about," Clisty said.

"You said no one else was around? But, there should have been hundreds, all over the church, the school and the grounds—janitors, secretaries, teachers ... and all the children." Emily's brow creased in worry.

"I remember, one of the men was shouting something about his wife leaving and taking his son," Becca offered.

"Which one?" Tears formed in Emily's eyes. "Oh ..." she moaned like one in grief. "It's all falling apart, isn't it?"

"What Emily? What's falling apart?" Clisty hoped she wouldn't frighten her. She needed a lot more information.

"Everything. Ezra said it might happen someday. He said ... if someone escapes ... if the truth gets out, it'll all fall like building blocks." Wiping tears from her eyes, she asked, "Who, who got out?"

What should she say? Clisty had run out of pretenses. "Emily ... Joselyn got out."

"You know where Joselyn is?" The woman drew her shaking fingers to her lips. "Tell me. I won't tell Ezra."

"We can take you there if you want to go with us," Jake offered. "But, we'd probably better hurry. Clisty has a deadline."

"I'll have to call Ezra and ask permission to leave the house," she responded with a timid, mousey voice. "I don't go anywhere without asking first."

"Would you like to see Joslyn and Pooky?' Clisty asked.

"Pooky too? Yes, yes!"

"I'm sorry, Emily," she added. "Joslyn and Pooky don't want to see Ezra, absolutely not!" She looked into Emily's eyes with a firm and resolute gaze. "And, we'd better get going."

"Alright, yes," Emily rattled on excitedly yet confused. "Let me remember. Ezra said if there's ever any trouble, I should get out and take all the papers with me."

"What papers?" Jake asked. "Are they easy to get to? We've gotta leave."

"They're in Ezra's office, in his safe."

"In his safe?" Clisty asked. Her eyes flashed to Jake's for silent confirmation. "They must be really important."

"Yes, they're the Temple records, financial papers and our own personal finances," she shared openly as she led the way into the office. "He said no one should get their hands on any of it."

Emily Treadway led the way from the living room to the elegant office, in the next room off the main entry. The large black safe sat inside a closet in the walnut paneled room. Everything about the space revealed Ezra's desire for control and power. Emily spun the dial carefully to the right and to the left several times, then pulled the handle down and opened it. The black, heavy steal-plated box was stuffed full of folders, portfolios, record ledgers, and papers. She pulled them all out, handed the tall stack to Jake and then reached to the back of the safe.

"Ezra said to be sure that I take every piece of gold and silver, every bank account book, and each off-shore banking record. My jewels are in the back." She pulled it all out. "I can't forget all of our credit cards and the passports." She grabbed a large black leather valise from the cabinet next to the safe and piled it all inside.

"Let's get out of here, now," Jake ordered.

"Wait, I'd better count," Emily said as she reached into the case. "Ezra would be furious ..." she looked at Clisty, "... and he could be dangerous if I don't have them all."

Clisty smiled and tried to move her along with her hand to Emily's elbow. "I understand. Let's hurry."

Emily pulled out five passport folders, and double counted. "Yes, three for Ezra and two for me."

Clisty and Jake just looked at each other, nodded and helped Emily with all the materials. *Move, move, move,* Clisty kept repeating to herself.

Becca picked up an armload of ledger books and as many loose papers as she could hold. "I've got these," she spoke out loud to those around her.

"Lock the safe again, Emily," Clisty reminded her. "Straighten everything up quickly."

Emily closed the safe, made sure everything was off the floor, and double checked again. When she seemed satisfied that she had taken care of everything as her husband would want her to, they all hurried out the front door and onto the porch.

"You'd better lock the door," Jake warned. "You can't be too careful."

Clisty knew the closed safe and locked door would slow Ezra for a few minutes. Perhaps he wouldn't suspect anything if all seemed in order. At least, it might stall him long enough for them to get out of sight before he realized what had happened.

Hoping to seem causal, Becca opened the double doors in the back of the van and all the papers were quickly stowed. They walked around to the side doors and piled in. Jake drove; Clisty rode beside him with the other three in the back. Jake didn't slam the van into gear or squeal the tires as he pulled away from the curb. He turned the key in the ignition, looked over his shoulder and slowly eased the van into the street. He wanted no eyes on them. To anyone who might have seen them, it would look like a small group of friends on an afternoon outing—no hurry, no worry.

Once the van began to roll, every head inside the vehicle turned and watched the street behind them. Jake drove the speed limit and watched for anyone in the rearview mirror. Hushed tones revealed the tension in the van that no one admitted. As they slowly turned the corner onto W. Devon Avenue, at the next cross street, an expensive SUV drove rapidly into the Treadway driveway. A man jumped out and nearly stumbled as he hurried toward the door. He didn't test the doorknob first. He tried to jam the key in the lock with shaking hands. Then, he dashed inside.

Emily stared out the window and gasped loudly as she and all those in the van disappeared around the corner. "He's back!"

Part V
Justice Sought - 1

"Let me out!" Emily Treadway yelled as the crew cleared the corner, her hands shaking as she reached for the handle of the van door.

"Emily, wait," Clisty soothed intently. "Becca will hold your hands until we stop. It could be dangerous if you opened the door while the van is moving." She looked at Clint. He was filming it all.

"Ezra will see that I'm gone! I shouldn't have left," Emily sobbed.

"I'll pull to the side of the road so we can talk," Jake offered in a smooth strong voice. "But, remember, the Freedom Temple has fallen. Ezra's scheme, he worked so hard to build over the years, is crumbling around him. He may be in a rage, looking for someone to blame. Our head start is to our advantage. Are you sure you want Ezra to catch up to us?"

"No, no, drive on!" She rubbed her hands across her eyes and buried her face in the palms. Her head suddenly popped up. "He'll search the house for me first, in the kitchen, upstairs in our bedroom, in Joslyn's room. He knows how much I've grieved since Joslyn and Pooky left." She looked at Clisty with fear in her eyes. "He won't have to go in the office though. When he sees I'm gone, he'll know. With the Temple abandoned, he'll be in escape mode."

"There weren't any other cars in your driveway at your house. There was no one else around," Jake observed. "Where were you supposed to meet him? How would you get there?"

"Ezra told me to put the files in a wheeled suitcase, but that was upstairs. So I took the valise. I know I did wrong," she sobbed. The others waited until she could pull herself together. "I was to walk to the Metro line, take the train into Chicago and meet him at the station there."

"So ... maybe he'll go to Chicago first, before starting a search elsewhere," Jake thought out loud.

"It will never occur to him that I won't be at the station," she said weakly. "I've never disobeyed him before." She wiped some more tears from her eyes. "It was poor Joslyn who got all the beatings for disobeying The Guardian."

Clisty's voice caught in her throat. "She was beaten?" Anger and grief rose up inside her.

"Many times," Emily whispered.

"Why didn't you stop him?" Clisty demanded. She tried very hard to not let her anger come through her voice. She was sure Emily would not cooperate with them if she became critical. Clisty suspected the woman had been criticized enough to last a lifetime.

"How could I stop him? He thought I rebelled one time because I had protected Joslyn. He twisted my arm until it broke." She rubbed her upper arm as pain-memory seemed to return. "He's big and he's strong."

"We can put you in a safe-house. We'll make the arrangements when we get home," Jake assured her.

"Where? Where is home?" Emily had turned again, her eyes fixed on the empty street behind them.

"Fort Wayne, Indiana," Becca said.

"Fort Wayne?" Her eyes brightened; her body straightened. "Will Joslyn and Pooky be there? Ezra adopted Joslyn in Fort Wayne and brought her home to me after our Rosie died," her eyes glazed as though she had drifted into her memories. "Ezra prayed and prayed that Rosie would live. When she didn't, he was never the same. He became mean and controlling. Why did God take her?"

"He didn't take her, Emily. He welcomed her," Clisty assured her with words she believed. As she thought, some pieces fell into place. "So ... you didn't know how Ezra came to adopt the child you called Joslyn?" she asked as she continued to build the news story and Jake's case.

"No," Emily whispered. "He said he called a friend in Chicago to go with him to Indiana because a little girl was ready to be adopted."

"It sounds like he was going to pick up a puppy," Clisty quipped sarcastically.

"Was his name, Melvin Dean Fargo?" Jake asked as he gripped the steering wheel.

"It's been so long ... he was a childhood friend of Ezra's. But, yes, I think that was his name."

"Do you know if Ezra has heard from Fargo in the last few days?" Jake asked.

"Yes and ... I thought it was strange. I don't think Ezra had heard from him in years. Melvin did call. He said he was in jail in Fort Wayne. I forgot that," Emily reported.

With fear and foreboding, Clisty watched dark clouds gather in the east, "Then, Ezra knows where Faith is."

• • • • •

They pulled into the parking lot of WFT at 5:30 p.m. Clisty had prepared for the six o'clock news before she left in the morning. A dress shirt, suit jacket and makeup kit waited in her office. "Becca, Clint," she said as she hopped out of the van, "we made it in time."

Jake got out and came around to Emily's door. "Mrs. Treadway, if it's alright with you, I'll take you with me to the police station where I'll arrange a safe-house location for you."

"Will Joslyn be there?" Emily asked.

"At police headquarters?" Clisty turned before going into the TV station.

"No," Emily said. "Will she be at the safe-house?"

Clisty looked at Jake for an answer. The wording had to be right. "She is safe someplace else," Jake explained. "We will make arrangements for you three to get together tomorrow, if Joslyn and Pooky want to see you."

"Why wouldn't they want to see me? She's my daughter and Pooky's my granddaughter." Emily's expression was confused. She seemed to be totally unaware of what Ezra and Fargo had done eighteen years ago.

"It isn't you, Emily. Fa— Joslyn has been very stressed emotionally for the last few days." She looked at Jake. "Emily, Joslyn had been held captive, as a hostage, by a bank robber during a standoff with the police. She was in the hospital for several days."

"Oh, dear God!' Emily gasped. "Is she alright?"

"Yes, well ... she's improving," Clisty said. "I have a newscast to report right now. Jake can take you to the police station and then the safe-house, and I'll be in contact with you soon, hopefully tomorrow. We'll need to give everyone a chance to think through the next move."

"You can watch Clisty's broadcast at the station while we set things up for you, if you want to," Jake offered.

"That would be nice. While we're at your police station, can you find a place to safeguard Ezra's papers? He wouldn't want me to lose any of them," she said. "If I can leave them with the police, that would be great."

"Jake and I will read them over and see if we can figure out what happened at the Temple," Clisty said casually. But, what she felt inside was a mixture of excitement and revenge. Mixed together, they frightened her.

• • • • •

"Today, the Mayor announced a new schedule for a vital spot in our community," Clisty spoke into the camera toward the end of the broadcast. "Beginning May 1, the Historic Old Fort will be open every Saturday from 2 pm to 4 pm through July. An influx of volunteer re-enactors and requests from the community, have made it possible."

"Any additional volunteers should contact the Historical Society," Dan Drummond added.

Clisty continued. "We are continuing to gather information regarding the suspect and the circumstances around the robbery of Fort Wayne Bank. The news crew and I traveled one-hundred sixty miles to investigate other threads to the story that began at the bank. As you know, there was a possible witness to the crime, who Melvin Dean Fargo later held as a hostage. The network has asked me to pursue the details and history of this young woman. That is what we began today. I will bring you her story when we have all the facts collected. In the meantime, we will protect the identity of that woman and the people around her. I am happy to say, she is home and cared for. We continue to uncovered important leads in the case and will report them as it is safe for all those involved. Be sure to tune in each evening. As we find information, we will bring it to you. Catch the first glimpse of our research on the News at Eleven. Thank you for watching. That's the early news from the Fort."

"Good job everyone," Becca announced. "Thanks for another great newscast."

Dan paused at the news desk. "Do I have to wait until eleven to hear what you found out today, too?"

"Yes," Clisty teased, "but that's only because we haven't planned what to say first, and on what schedule we'll release it. This whole thing has grown far beyond what we knew we would find so quickly."

"You had a three hour drive back to Indiana. Did you all sleep?" he joked.

"No, we had someone with us. The wife of the man who kidnapped Faith was in the van during the entire trip. It appears she didn't know anything about the whole thing. She thought her husband had come to Indiana, all those years ago, to adopt a girl to replace the daughter they had just lost. I don't know what kind of person she was before she met Ezra Treadway, but, right now, she is an empty shell. She only does what he tells her to do and only goes where she has asked permission to go. She doesn't drive. She doesn't even answer the phone at home unless the caller ID shows it's her husband."

"What? How can that be?" Dan shook his head. "What century does she live in?"

"Emily lives in the Century of Ezra and Ezra's whole world is about him." Clisty removed her lapel mic and stood up. "She is so fragile we couldn't discuss the case in front of her. Becca is coming over to my apartment and we'll write the news story for tonight." She stopped and turned back to Dan. "There are many twists in this story and we've already turned a very dangerous corner. Please ... say a prayer for us."

• • • • •

"Come in, Becca," Clisty said. "Jake will be here in a few minutes. We have to know what we can report before Ezra is caught. We can't accidently give him information that would aid him in finding Emily, Faith and Pooky."

146

"Clisty, that's right. We have to balance our news story with the Prosecutor's ability to nail this guy."

"We're investigating the story and have every right to report it. But, Becca ..." Clisty wrung her hands, "I want him caught so bad I can't stand it."

The door buzzer rang. "If you'll make some coffee, I'll get Jake," Becca offered.

"Sure," Clisty agreed and had the pot on by the time Jake had his jacket off. "Go ahead and sit down. I'll be right over," she said.

She got some mugs out of the cabinet and smiled. Her dirty cup from breakfast and cereal bowl still sat on the black granite counter. A week ago, she wouldn't have been able to tolerate dirty dishes anywhere. Something or someone was freeing her from her obsessions. "You like a little milk in your coffee, right?" she asked Becca.

"Right."

"Hi Babe," Jake went over and kissed Clisty on the neck while her head was down preparing the cups.

"I'll spill this stuff if you keep that up," she laughed.

"I'll clean it up," he joked. "It'll be worth it."

"Hey, you two," Becca teased, "save the play for later."

Clisty was embarrassed and felt her cheeks grow warm. Carrying Becca's cup to the conversation area, she tried to shake off her self-consciousness and nearly spilled the coffee. "Here," she handed Becca the cup. "Let's get busy. I'll get you a napkin. I splashed a little."

"That's okay. Oh, I forgot, you don't want a drop on your table," Becca apologized.

"Don't worry about it," Clisty said as she wiped up the spot and left the crumpled napkin on the table. She looked at it there on her high-shine polished table and laughed to herself.

"First, how long do you want the segment for the eleven o'clock news?" Jake asked. "And, do you plan to use any of the video Clint shot today?"

"Let's back up," Clisty began. "I was thinking about all of this in the van on the way home. There are several stories here that are interconnected. There's the bank robbery; Faith's kidnapping; Fargo's connection to Ezra; the abuses at the Treadway home; and the corruption at the Freedom Temple."

Jake took out his small notebook and pen. "Actually, there are only two cases we have jurisdiction over—Ezra's involvement in the bank robbery and Faith's kidnapping. The other offences will be charges in Illinois since that is where they happened."

"I hadn't thought about that," Clisty whispered.

"First, we have to keep Faith, Pooky and Emily safe," Jake began. "For now, Emily is being settled into a safe-house. She'll have an officer with her at all times. Faith and Pooky are at the Sterlings' home." He thought for a moment and then added, "I would think it best for you not to show pictures of Ezra or Emily on the newscast. I can't tell you what to do, freedom of the press and all. Maybe Ezra will think that our case is still about Fargo, his bank robbery and holding Faith as a hostage at the time of the police standoff."

"Okay," Clisty processed, "If we focus on Fargo for tonight's broadcast, we can use the pictures of Chicago Clint took as we drove through. We can ask questions more than give answers for tonight's broadcast."

"Right," Becca agreed and opened the e-tablet she had brought. "Why was this Chicago resident, Fargo, in Fort Wayne?"

"Did he know the woman he held captive before coming to Indiana?" Clisty added to the list.

"Was there any connection between Fargo and Faith's abduction eighteen years ago?" Jake offered.

Clisty looked up from her thoughts, "Will that jeopardize your other charges and investigations?"

"No," he answered. "We already know he's connected by helping Ezra abduct her long ago. You don't have to get ahead of the story. You can ask the question."

"That helps, Jake, thanks," Clisty said. "We can show the clip of Fargo coming out of the house behind Faith. Becca, please write this down. 'We went to Chicago seeking information about the bank robbery suspect, Melvin Dean Fargo.' Then, we show the clip of the city and some of the scenery from Fort Wayne to Chicago. Next, we ask our questions." She tapped her fingers on her knees. "That's a beginning."

"Great," Becca continued to enter data and smiled. "The video showing the burning of the Freedom Temple that came in from the NCC station can wait for the entire News magazine story to be completed."

"That sounds good," Clisty began, and then slowly formed a new thought. "Jake, Indiana can't charge Treadway for crimes in Illinois, but can we dig up the information and present whatever we find in the final broadcast?"

"If you're careful, you don't want to taint the jury that will hear the case over in Illinois. If you document all your findings I would think that would be alright."

"I didn't think about that," she drew out slowly. "We have the material that Emily had you lock away in the police station. We'll comb through all of that and develop a second Heartland story, centered on the charges in Illinois." She jumped up and paced back and forth. "We haven't even started yet and we already have two great programs for *Stories from the Heartland*."

$\mathcal{V}$

Justice Sought – 2

"Okay, Becca," Clisty spoke into her cell phone as she made arrangements the next morning to meet Becca and Clint at the safe-house. "It's," she checked her watch, "quarter 'til ten. I'm ready, so why don't you two stop by here and pick me up?"

"What about arranging a meeting?" Becca asked. "When do you want Faith and Emily to see each other again?"

"It's not up to me. It's up to Faith." Story or not, Clisty was certain of that point. "Faith will not be pushed into anything."

"I know ... but it would make great TV," Becca said.

"Rebecca, that's a terrible thing to say," then, she laughed. "I know what you mean. Better yet, meet me at the Sterlings' house. Say, about 10:30 am. That will give me a chance to break the news to Faith and the Sterlings that we brought Emily Treadway back with us. Roma and Ralph lost a lot, too. Faith lost her childhood and her parents lost living that childhood with her."

"Got ya," Becca agreed. "Ten thirty it is."

• • • • •

"Come in Clisty," Roma opened her front door and gave Clisty a hug. "Ralph's in the kitchen getting coffee. You want some?"

"Sure ... always," she said. She wanted to sound upbeat; after all, they had been to Illinois and back and had gathered a lot of information. But, she couldn't set a positive tone with her voice.

"I have this small camera," she said as she pulled it from her bag. "It will record sound as well," she pressed the "on" button. "With your permission, and of course, Faith's too, I'd like to record our conversation. I have turned it on to record your answer to my request to film."

"Yes, I suppose it's okay, if it's alright with Faith." She stopped and studied Clisty for a second. "Has something else happened?" Roma asked.

"No ... yes, there could be," Clisty said as she took the cup Ralph offered.

"What's wrong?" Roma put her hand to her chest.

"Where are Faith and Pooky?" Clisty asked quietly, like she was sharing a secret.

"They're in the back yard," Ralph's muscles tightened and he appeared tense. "It sounds like something's going on."

"Jake and the crew and I went over to Illinois yesterday," she started.

"Yes, we saw it on the eleven o'clock news last evening," he said, sat down and placed his cup on the table beside him. "What are you not telling us?"

"I'm not going to keep anything from you. Any secrecy you hear or see on the news, is so Faith and Pooky are safe. Any withholding of information is so the perpetrator can't find out the details." She sipped her coffee. "We found the Freedom Temple and ... we found Lady, the woman who acted as Faith's mother. Her name is Emily Treadway."

"Oh, my goodness," Roma gasped as she covered her face with her hands. Then, she snapped her attention back to Clisty, "And?"

"And ... she's here. We brought her back to Fort Wayne with us." Clisty tried to find a way to say it but the truth was all she had. "We had to. She wasn't safe in Illinois," Clisty paused and tried to carefully gather her next words. "Of course she wants to see Faith and Pooky, but it is entirely up to Faith."

"No," Roma stated fiercely, "it's up to me."

"Maybe—"Clisty tried to offer an acceptable scenario.

"I said no. That woman has had her for eighteen years. I only got her for nine." She closed her eyes and shook her head. "No!"

"No what?" Faith asked as she and Pooky came in through the dining room. She looked at the three and grabbed the back of a chair and guessed, "Something's happened."

Roma looked at Faith's fear-etched face. "You'd better tell her, Clisty. She'll only retreat into her nightmares and constant vigilance if she doesn't know what you found out."

"Mama," Faith grabbed Pooky and drew her close. "What's wrong?"

Roma sat in a wing back chair and gestured to Faith. "Come Honey, you and Pooky sit down."

Faith slowly sank onto the sofa and pulled Pooky down next to her. "What is it?"

"Faith ...," Clisty began, "first of all, I have a camera turned on to record our conversation. If you don't want me to record, I'll turn it off. What I'm about to say, will greatly enhance your story as I report it on the *Stories from the Heartland* series, and it could help the Prosecutor's case."

"Okay, then go ahead and record it. Can I tell you to stop later if I'm uncomfortable with it?" Faith kept her eyes on the camera.

"Yes, of course. You can get up and step out of the room if you need a break. Faith, you are free to do anything you want to do," Clisty said.

"Then, let's go. You three were talking when I came into the room. Something has happened. What?" Faith was quietly assertive and pointed in her question. She soon ignored the camera.

"Jake, Clint the cameraman, Becca and I went to Illinois yesterday," Clisty began.

"Illinois?" Pooky grabbed Faith's arm, squeezed her eyes shut and hung on. "My school was in Illinois."

"Yes, Pooky," Clisty said. "I know. We visited your school. Your principal, Mr. Mitchel, said he remembers you."

"Clisty, why?" Faith questioned with an accusation in her voice. "Why did you go there?"

"Please, listen to me. You need to hear it all." Clisty explained the entire previous day, all that they saw and all they heard. "Faith, I don't think Lady knew that you had been kidnapped. She told us she believed that Ezra had adopted you. She seems to believe everything he says."

"Ezra?" Faith asked. She looked confused again. "Who is Ezra?"

"The Guardian, Faith. The Guardian's name is Ezra Treadway." Clisty watched Faith's expression change from intent listening to confusion. "We snuck into the Freedom Temple and heard Ezra and a couple of other men, talking about the Freedom Temple's crash and how everyone else had left the cult."

"The Freedom Temple?" Faith asked.

Clisty tried to pull together all the details she had dumped on Faith. "Remember, I told you—"

"I know," Faith admitted. Her eyes were down like she was escaping inside herself. "I just wish I didn't know." She looked up. "I'm not damaged, Clisty. I'm only confused because I've been isolated for so long. I knew nothing of the world around me or beyond my walls. A few times I saw the local news but usually, they cut off the electricity to my room during the news hour. I never knew why, until now."

"Faith, we brought the woman, Lady you called her, back here with us." Clisty watched as Faith's face drew up in pain as the news of her own life wounded her over and over. "Her name is Emily Treadway. She'd like to see you and Pooky. I told her you would decide if you want to see her."

"Faith Treadway," she repeated slowly. "I didn't know my name." Her eyes filled with tears.

Roma wrapped her arms tightly around her own body and rocked back and forth. "You never knew your own name?" Roma choked between her tears.

"They said I wasn't going anywhere so I didn't need to have a second name," Faith whispered.

"When you got married," her father asked, "didn't Steven tell you your name, or call you, Mrs. Somebody?" His jaw worked in anger; his fists clenched.

"He didn't disobey his father ... ever. He wanted to be able to leave the house, go to work and school. Freedom would have stopped if he had done anything The Guardian forbad." Tears rolled down her face.

Pooky started to smile, "Mama, I didn't know we had another name." Then, suddenly her joy fell to the floor and panic took over. Her gaze followed something that moved slowly outside, from left to right. Her eyes grew large and full of alarm.

Faith was not facing the front porch directly. She jerked around to see what had frightened Pooky and screamed a terror stricken sound that filled the house. Roma and Ralph jumped up, turned and looked to the front door. The beveled glass window could not keep out the evil that lurked there, as Ezra Treadway burst through, welding a Glock 27. He waved the firearm in the air erratically; the red laser dot flew from forehead, to wall, to floor. His eyes blazed with rage and then, Clisty remembered. She knew exactly who he was, even after eighteen years. He had stabbed a permanent tattoo of horror on her mind. She jumped to her feet.

"Sit down, now!" Treadway shouted, pointed the weapon at each one and took a few more steps into the house. "I said sit down—do it!" he growled again.

Clisty sat down, fearfully sitting on the edge of her seat. Each of them did not take their eyes off the raging bull in their midst. Clisty's mind raced. How could she get word to Jake, to anyone? Becca and Clint would be there soon. They would be in danger, too. She felt her phone in her pocket. If she tried to save them all and pull it out, a bullet might be her reward. She caught Ralph's eye but saw no remedy there.

"You have everything of mine!" Treadway growled and paced back and forth. He grabbed the top of his head like he was afraid it would explode and waved the gun wildly. "You have my wife, my daughter, my granddaughter, and all of my personal papers. I want them ... all," he ordered. "Pooky, come over here," he yelled and reached out an arm for her.

"No, Grandpa! No!" she sobbed and buried her head in her mother's shoulder.

"No, Guardian! You're terrifying her," Faith yelled back and clutched her daughter.

"This is your doing, Jocelyn!" he ranted, his large body puffed out and menacing. The gun wobbled in his panic-driven hands. "You were nothing but trouble from the day I brought you home."

Pooky raised her head; her angry eyes flashed as she jumped up and lunged in Ezra's direction. "Maybe she didn't want to stay with you," she screamed. "You're mean!"

Ezra raised his left hand and, with a wide sweep, smacked Pooky across the face and knocked her to the floor. She slid across the tile, four feet away. Turning, he pointed the Glock at her, the laser beaded on her chest, "You little brat! Haven't you learned anything yet?"

His frantic flailing about caused his entire body to follow his aggression. Faith jumped to her feet the minute Ezra's eyes no longer locked on her. With his focus on Pooky, Faith picked up Roma's heavy, leaded crystal vase from the table and swung it up the side of Ezra's head. He fell to the ground like downed timber, cracking his head on a bookcase on the way down. Faith frantically stepped over him and picked Pooky up, soothing her hysterical sobs.

Faith!" Clisty shouted in fear and apprehension pointing to Ezra.

"He's still moving. Hit him again," Ralph yelled and jumped up, his arm making phantom jabs in the air.

"No," Faith refused, but could not take her eyes off him. "I'll get his gun," she said as she dropped Pooky in Roma's lap and moved in Ezra's direction. She let the vase fall to the floor.

"No!" they all gasped.

"It's too dangerous!" Roma pleaded.

"Stay away from him." Ralph yelled and started to stand.

Clisty lunged, jerked up the vase and held it in striking position over Treadway. "You better not move," she hissed.

Faith yelled, "I am free and I'll stay free!" She stepped past the moaning body of The Guardian and toward the Glock.

The gun, knocked out of Ezra's hand, had slid across the entry tile. Faith dove for it, rolled on the floor, picked it up and shuddered. With trembling hands she pointed the weapon at her tormentor and captor, the laser focused a red beam on his head.

"I've got him, Faith," Jake said firmly and calmly as he burst through the door. He took Treadway's gun from Faith's hand, slipped it in his belt and pulled out his handcuffs. They all watched in stunned silence.

"She was only protecting us," they all said.

"These cuffs aren't for Faith. They're for Treadway," Jake growled. He forced the man's hands behind his back and slapped the cuffs on him. "We have many charges for this guy," he said roughly and inspected Ezra's head for the wound he had received.

"Some of us went over the files Emily gave us. This man will have a whole list of charges against him, some in Indiana and some in Illinois."

As Ezra come to, Jake checked his pupillary reaction for responsiveness. "Ezra Treadway, you are under arrest for the kidnapping of Faith Sterling and the attempted abduction of Clisty Sinclair." He got the man to his feet and continued. "And, that's just for a start. You have the right to remain silent," he continued quoting his Miranda rights to Treadway.

Clisty saw Clint filming through the porch window and wondered how long he had been standing there. Becca waited beside him, her hand over her mouth, fear on her face. Squealing tires and the sound of pounding shoes on the porch announced a heavily armed police back-up force had arrived.

"Take him in," Jake directed the uniformed officers. "He's been Mirandized. Do everything by the book." He glared at Treadway. "You're not getting out of anything." The officers took custody of him and led him out of the house.

"Jake, how did you know?" Clisty jumped up.

"You told Becca to meet you here. They arrived in time to see Treadway burst through the door. Becca called me while Clint filmed."

"That will be our News at Eleven," Clisty said. "Maybe not tonight, but it will make the cut for the full story in the news magazine." It didn't matter to Clisty if they held the video for several days or used it that evening. Treadway had met his match. She and Faith were no longer two little nine year old girls, but independent women who had waited eighteen years to capture the monster of their nightmares.

V

Justice Sought - 3

"Oh," Clisty grabbed Jake's arm as her legs wilted under her.

"Are you alright?" Jake asked and put his arm around her before leaving Ralph and Roma's house. He leaned over and kissed the top of her head.

"I'm okay, I guess. But, I feel like I'm rattling inside." Clisty felt safe in Jake's arms. All of the fear and adrenalin rush had reached its peak inside her mind and body, and hadn't yet slipped down anywhere near a normal range. She didn't want him to leave.

"You've experienced a traumatic event, Honey. Not many people have a Glock's laser beam zeroed in on their forehead, especially not in a town where the only target is within the goal zone on the ice at the Coliseum. You're going to be rattled for a while, shaken but not broken." While still holding her in his arms, he rubbed her back and breathed with her, gradually slowing his pace, which steadied her panic-breathing.

While Jake comforted Clisty, Roma and Ralph reached out to Faith and Pooky. Becca directed Clint to film the moment.

"I've gotta go," Jake whispered. "I need to start the interrogation and begin the paper work." He kissed the top of her head. "Have dinner with me at seven?"

"Absolutely," Clisty reached up and kissed him. It felt good to be open about the feelings she had hidden from herself and others. She felt released from the love-phobia, as she called it in her quiet moments alone, released from the need to control everything and everyone close to her. Would it last? Would control dictate her new position with the network, or would love finally win?

"Absolutely," he winked and it sent a warm ripple down Clisty's body. She knew his response had nothing to do with supper.

Becca placed Clint to the side of the group where he could get an angle shot on everyone. "Is everyone okay?" she asked. "As the producer, I'd like to film the debriefing we need to do now. But," she turned to Faith, "it is all up to you, Faith. I will not push you in any way."

"I think we're all okay," Roma answered. "Faith, if you want to tell everyone what happened today, yesterday and all the yesterdays we lost, that is up to you. Talking about it might help you release some demons that continue to hold you captive. I will support anything you choose. And, yes, my dear, you do have choices."

"Choices ... wow. I have choices. I can't remember having a choice in anything. Not since Clisty and I tried to decide which bike path to take to the park. It feels like I can stand up a little taller. Or, ride a little farther," Faith exhaled heavily, slowly and smiled at Clisty. She sat on one of the side chairs and pulled Pooky onto her lap.

"You were both very brave today," Roma said as she went to them and kissed their cheeks.

"Okay, Clint," Becca directed, "you can film. As much as you can, Faith, just ignore the camera ... you too, Pooky."

Clisty sat on the couch and leaned her hands on her knees. "Faith, when you first came back to Fort Wayne, you were nearly empty, helpless, hopeless, and weak. Today, you were on the attack. How did all that change so fast for you?"

"I could feel the difference. When I was in that other house, in that other town ... what did you call it?"

Clisty looked at Roma and Ralph. Baffled by so many inconsistencies, she struggled to understand Faith's word-gaps. "Naperville, Faith. You lived in Naperville for eighteen years." She shook her head as she tried to understand.

"I was never in Naperville, though," Faith reminded her. "I was never out of my upstairs room, then two rooms with Steven, except an occasional meal downstairs. When I left the black house, I was completely confused, disoriented, lost, both emotionally and physically. I had just lost Steven." She smiled at Pooky. "But, today, The Guardian hit my daughter. A mother will fight back."

"A mother-cat on the attack," Clisty said and smiled at her friend's strength. "Now, back to the events of your escape ... how did you know what direction to go when you got to the end of the sidewalk outside your front door?" Clisty asked.

"I didn't. Steven had driven Pooky to school for two weeks, and he had gone the same way each time. She remembered how to get to the highway. I like to think her daddy was showing her the way out."

Clisty was proud of Pooky. "You helped save yourself and your mom, Pooky. You remind me of your mother when she was your age. Full of adventure, ready to take on the world."

"I do?" Pooky asked with wide, smiling eyes.

"You sure do." Clisty thought for a moment and directed a question to her. "Pooky, your grandma and I haven't been with your mom for a long time. Have you ever seen her act with such courage before?"

"Sure. She was always talking back to The Guardian—to Grandpa. He used to hit her for not minding him or for sassing him, but she never cried. It scared me, though." Pooky started to cover her face, and then she grabbed her mother's arm and squeezed it as those memories still seemed to have the power to frighten her.

"Why do you think she sassed him?" Clisty asked while Clint adjusted the lens for a close up.

"Daddy was so sick and The Guardian wouldn't call the doctor. Daddy kept holding his chest. He wrinkled up his face and it looked like he hurt. I cried, but Mama screamed at Grandpa." Pooky's eyes filled with tears.

"Did your daddy get well?" Clisty asked, while Pooky's grandparents showed their own sorrow.

"No. Grandpa said to pray for him. He said if Mama didn't pray hard enough, Daddy would die and it would be her fault." Pooky collapsed in Faith's arms. "Daddy died," she sobbed.

"You both know it wasn't your mother's fault, don't you?" Clisty asked with an edge of anger to her voice. She could not understand how anyone could put so much guilt on someone else, especially a child.

"I know," Pooky looked up. "It was The Guardian's fault!"

"Do you accept that, Faith? Do you know it wasn't your fault?"

"I know it wasn't my fault," Faith said as she smiled. "Mama Roma taught me to pray and she prayed with me since I was a baby," she smiled at her mother. "I know how to pray. God must have had other plans for Steven, other than mine."

"Why didn't you go to his funeral, Faith?" Clisty continued her interview.

"I was never allowed to leave the house. The funeral was just one more place I couldn't go to, as far as The Guardian was concerned. But, it would have meant a lot to Pooky and me if we could have said our goodbyes."

Clisty knew she had to ask the hard question. "Faith, for your trip back to Indiana, how did you happen to accept a ride from Melvin Dean Fargo, of all people?"

"Because, of all the people, his was the only face I recognized. In the whole world outside the stone house, there was only one face that looked familiar to me. It was Melvin Dean Fargo's face. Pooky and I had walked up to the main road and saw a filling station. There was a man inside a pickup truck, and I recognized him. I didn't know how I knew him. He just seemed familiar. I asked him if he was going to Indiana and if we could ride. He said okay, but first he'd have to make a phone call. He called from a small phone in his hand but he said no one was home," Faith recalled, as if she saw the pictures in her head.

"He may have been calling Treadway, but his cell phone would have been off due to the funeral," Clisty said as she began to put some of the threads together.

"He tried to call several more times." Then she remembered he had talked to her a little. "'Do you have any money?' he asked. I said no, we have nothing. He said, 'Then, I'll have to go to the bank again in a few days? I have the new directions.'"

"Again?" Clisty asked. "Are you sure he said, 'again'?"

"I heard him too," Pooky assured her. "I know he said, 'again.'"

"Do you remember having seen Fargo before?" Clisty hoped to pull another piece of the case out of the back of Faith's memory. Each clue seemed to reach like centipede legs back to the original kidnapping, so long ago.

"No, I just knew he looked familiar," she said with growing confidence.

"Faith, Emily Treadway, the woman you called Lady, would like to see you and Pooky. The important thing is, are you ready to see her?" Clisty looked from Faith to Roma. She hoped she had not alienated Roma, a solid supporter of the Heartland story. The full telling of the tale expanded far beyond the bank robbery. "Roma, what do you think?"

"Faith ..." Roma started slowly, "this morning, I've seen how strong you have become. It sounds like you always were—standing up to Treadway." She took Ralph's hand. "Here in our home, your home, you are free to go anywhere you want to go. And ... if you want to see Emily and if you want us to meet her, your dad and I can go with you."

Faith took a deep breath and words tumbled out. "Yes, oh please, yes. That would be wonderful." She stopped and rubbed her hands together. "Mama, I have to make you believe that I always called that woman, Lady. You were, and always be, my only mother, my mama. I thought about you and Daddy every day of my life."

• • • • •

"Thank you for arranging our meeting with Emily Treadway, Detective Davis," Clisty spoke into the camera in a conference room at the police station. "As we have reported over the last few evenings, our story began when the image of Faith Sterling appeared on the ATM surveillance camera outside Fort Wayne Bank. Recognized as the woman kidnapped from Fort Wayne at nine years of age by Ezra Treadway, Faith Sterling escaped and made her way back home. Melvin Dean Fargo, the self-confessed robber of Fort Wayne Bank, was the accomplice to the kidnapping and was a friend of Treadway's. Faith lived in Illinois as the captive-daughter of Ezra and Emily Treadway." Clisty walked over to the large table. "We have met here today in a neutral setting so Faith can have the opportunity to confront Emily Treadway. She is the person Faith called 'Lady' the entire eighteen years the Treadways held her captive. Faith's parents, Ralph and Roma Sterling will be with her. They will all join us in a moment." Clisty turned from the camera to Emily.

Clisty sat down and faced the woman on the other side of the table. Though she, Jake and the others had brought Emily to Indiana, the woman remained a stranger. "Thank you for coming, Mrs. Treadway. I know you have wanted to see Faith and her daughter since you came to Fort Wayne. Will you tell the audience what you called Faith during the years she lived in your home?" Clisty was warm yet professional.

"We called Faith, Joselyn. Of course I wanted to see her. She's my daughter," Emily stated with a sweet smile on her face.

"I understand that's what you think, Mrs. Treadway," Clisty said firmly. "You do know, however, if you call Faith, 'your daughter,' or use the name, 'Jocelyn,' she will leave the room."

Emily looked down at the table. "Yes, I hear you."

Clisty was ready when Jake brought Roma and Ralph into the room. "Mrs. Treadway, Faith wanted her parents to be with her. They have come in first so you can meet them before their daughter comes in. This is Roma and Ralph Sterling."

Emily looked at both of them, her mouth open in apparent surprise. Stunned, she said nothing at first and then stood. "I ... am so sorry." She started to explain. "I didn't know. I didn't know that Joselyn had living parents ... that she had been kidnapped."

"We understand that," Ralph said, his body tense. "Her name is Faith. It always has been. Faith was kidnapped; Faith was missing; and, Faith has returned, on her own, not from anything you did to help her." He and Roma sat down at the end of the table. Jake leaned against the wall, an observer, not an interrogator.

"Yes, Mr. Sterling," Emily spoke with humility. "I am sorry to say, I agree. I didn't help her," she hung her head and didn't make eye contact, "even though she told me she had parents in Fort Wayne."

"You knew?" Roma lunged in the woman's direction. Ralph tugged gently on Roma's shirt sleeve and patted her back as she settled again in her chair.

"Yes, I knew what the child told me, but my husband said something else." Her body grew tense and she wrung her hands. "I didn't know who to believe and," she whispered, "I wanted to keep her."

Jake opened the conference room door. "Are you ready for Faith?"

"I don't know," Clisty spoke with control and authority. "You all tell me. Are you ready for Faith to come in? I will demand that she not be upset or I will shut this meeting down. Any uproar might make good TV, but I will not permit it at Faith's expense."

"Yes, yes," Emily begged. "Please, don't blame me for Ezra's crimes. I was his captive, too. Now, I just want to see her." Her voice broke under the emotion that was evident in her tears.

"Alright," Roma answered and stared at the broken woman beside her.

Faith came in the room, hesitantly. She looked at her parents and then at Emily. "Mama, Daddy," she said as she sat opposite Emily and beside her parents. "Lady," she nodded an acknowledgement. "Are you alright?"

"I'm okay, Jos—" she stopped quickly, "Faith. Are you okay? How is Pooky?"

"She's fine. She wants to see you." Faith twisted a childhood handkerchief she held in her hands. Embroidered little red roses were in one corner, a symbol from her lost childhood she could hold on to.

"Pooky wants to see me?" Emily started to reach for Faith's hands then pulled back. "Faith," she looked at the woman she had called daughter for eighteen years, "I want you to know, I had absolutely no idea that Ezra had kidnapped you. He told me he had adopted you."

"I told you!" Faith whispered forcefully. "Why didn't you believe me? Why did you pretend to love me but not let me call you Mom? Why did I have to call you Lady?" Faith had sadness in her voice, not anger.

Those were surprising emotions to Clisty. She didn't think she was past the anger herself and she had only lived the memory. Faith had lived the tragedy.

"You wanted to call her Mom or Mother?' Clisty asked.

"Not Mother. I had a mother. And, not Mama," she looked at Roma and took her hand. "But, I needed to have someone who claimed me. I needed a mom, even if she wasn't really my mom."

"I know, Faith. You're right," Emily admitted. "Lady was all you could call me. Ezra said I had to keep a wall between us. He said you might die like our first daughter did. He said it wouldn't hurt as much if it happened again, if we didn't get close to you. Ezra was so controlling. He controlled you, me, Steven, everyone and everything."

"Was I actually married to Steven?" Faith asked, shaking her head in disbelief. "Lady, I had no last name."

"Yes, Ezra had a license to marry people. You and Steven were married and your marriage license was filed and recorded properly."

"Did I sign it? I don't remember," Faith shook her head in frustration and confusion.

"Yes, you signed it," Emily said. "Don't you remember? Ezra always had a way of manipulating people so they didn't know what they were doing. You signed, *Joselyn* and then Ezra spilled some water on the document. He said, 'That's okay. When it's dry, you can finish it.' He put it in his office and signed Treadway for you the next day and mailed it in."

"But my name has never been Joselyn Treadway. The wrong name is on my marriage license," Faith put her head in her hands and leaned on the table. "If the authorities agree that I was Joselyn Treadway at the time I signed the marriage license, then would my real name be Joselyn or Faith Treadway. Is it all a lie?"

"We'll contact our attorney the first time his office is open, and see if we can get it all straightened out," her dad assured her. "You loved Steven and Pooky loved her daddy. That's all you need to know now. None of that is a lie, Faith."

"Thank you, Mr. Sterling," Emily said as she turned to them. "That means a lot to me that Steven is honored. He loved them both so much." Again she had to blot tears from her eyes.

"It's not for you, Ma'am,' Ralph barked. "It's for the girls."

"I know," Emily said apologetically.

The door opened a crack and a small voice came from the other side. "Can I come in?" Pooky asked softly as she stuck her head through the opening.

"Are we ready for the little miss?" Clisty asked Faith.

"Sure," Faith said as she turned around and reached out her arms to her daughter. "Come on in, Honey."

Pooky hugged her mom and sat down beside her. She looked over, on the other side of Faith, at the Sterlings. "Grandma!" she squealed, jumped up, ran around and embraced her. She stepped back a little, still holding on to Roma. "Did you see her? My other grandma is here, too."

"Yes," Roma answered her granddaughter. "We've been talking."

"Do I have to hate her? I will if you want me to," she asked with probing eyes. "Or, is it okay if I love her, too?" Pooky asked without turning toward Emily. "'Cause if I'm supposed to hate her, I'll pretend she isn't here."

Roma choked and cleared her throat as tears streamed down her face. "There has been enough living like a ghost, Baby. It's like people look right through you," she patted Pooky's cheek. "Yes, Sweetheart, as long as your Grandma Emily loves you and treats you right, it is perfectly alright for you to love her, too. We can never have too many people in our lives who love us."

"Oh, good," Pooky squealed as she ran to Emily and threw her arms around her. "I missed you, Grandma."

Emily could not control her emotions and dropped her head onto Pooky's shoulder. "I missed you too, Baby," she cried.

Faith smiled at the closeness of her daughter and Lady. She didn't join in the embrace. Instead, she got up, went around behind her own parents and embraced them with eighteen years' worth of love.

"Cut, I think that's enough for now," Becca said as she wiped her own eyes.

As soon as the filming stopped, Clisty's phone rang. She looked at the screen and decided she needed to take the call. She got up from the table, went over to the window and put a finger to her free ear. "Hello, Clisty Sinclair."

"This is Bradley Funderbird in New York," a voice said. "Your local station just connected the interview you had with Faith, her parents and Mrs. Treadway with us here at the network office."

"Oh yes. Becca was hoping that the feed would be able to reach you without actually broadcasting at this time," Clisty said. "How did it come through?"

"It was great. Our offer to you is firm. Regardless of how Ezra Treadway's trial turns out, and we do want you to be there to report it, we are offering you a weekly segment on our Network News Magazine, titled, *Stories from the Heartland*. We would feed story ideas to you that come in to our New York office from the middle of the country, with an emphasis on wholesome, upbeat, down-to-earth people and how they manage to overcome the difficulties that are present in today's society."

"Sir," she gasped, "that is wonderful." She looked at Jake, "Can you give me a little while to decide?"

"Of course. I'll have to admit, I don't know what you have to decide. This is a promotion, Clisty. You have to seize the opportunity when it comes. It may not come again."

"I know, Sir, but so much has happened." Clisty studied Faith's face and looked again at Jake. She had been afraid to love and let people get close enough for her to experience messy, complicated relationships since Faith disappeared. Now Faith was back and Clisty's emotions were set free to experience feelings she wondered if she would ever have. With Jake, maybe—

"I think a good time to respond would be after Treadway's trial," Funderbird said with a voice of authority. "That will wrap up that first network story you are doing. Here in New York, we'll start gathering the story leads. The segments will run, with you or with someone else, Clisty."

"I understand. Thank you, Mr. Funderbird," she said as she looked up and saw Jake listening to her end of the conversation. "Please, go ahead and send the ideas as you receive them. I would like to have the opportunity to see if I can relate to any of them."

"I certainly will do that, Clisty," Funderbird said. Clisty pressed "end call" on her screen.

Jake threw his hand to his chest in a disclaiming gesture. "I was not eavesdropping, Babe. You were talking in front of us and—"

"Honey," Clisty laughed," I know you weren't trying to listen in on my conversation. You couldn't help but hear it."

"Funderbird? Interesting name. Who's he, if I may ask?"

"That's okay." She leaned into Jake and rested her head on his chest. "Bradley Funderbird is the president of the network."

"In New York?"

"In New York City," she said and kissed his cheek.

V

Justice Sought - 4

"We are outside the courtroom just minutes before the trial of Ezra Treadway will begin." Clisty stood in front of the camera in the hall with large, closed wooden courtroom doors behind her. "The judge has ruled against television cameras inside the courtroom. However, he does allow reporters. I'll take notes and sketch the scene as I see it. They may look like stick figures to another artist, but I'll do my best to bring the story as accurately as possible."

Inside the courtroom, the bailiff positioned himself in front of the court. "All rise," he announced.

"I need to take my seat," Clisty signed off, opened the door, hurried midway up the isle and sat down beside Roma and Ralph just as all those present took their seats. She opened her e-tablet and poised her hands to list the charges.

The bailiff read the charges against Ezra Treadway. Clisty quickly brought up the meaning of each charge on her touch screen. She always did her research completely and well in advance of a hearing. That research came up immediately on Clisty's tablet and she followed the words as the bailiff spoke.

"Kidnapping and/or Criminal Confinement:" Indiana Code – Section 35-42-3-3 Criminal Confinement:

    a.   A person who knowingly or intentionally:

        (1) confines another person without the person's consent;

(2) or, removes another person by fraud, enticement, force, or threat of force, from one (1) place to another; commits criminal confinement. Except as provided in subsection (b), the offense of criminal confinement is a Class D felony.

  (a) The offense of criminal confinement defined in subsection (a) is:

  (1) A Class C felony if:

      (A) The person confined or removed is less than fourteen (14) years of age and is not the confining or removing person's child;
      (B) It is committed by using a vehicle;

"Got ya!" she screamed inside, her hand pumping a fist in triumph. Clisty brought up her notes for the next charge.

"Accessory to Robbery."

"Those who aid in the commission of a crime before or after the actual act are called accessories to the crime. Any person, who willingly and intentionally helps a person before a crime is committed, is considered an accessory before the fact. For example, the person who provides the principle with maps of the bank, security information, and other details may be considered an accessory before the fact.

"That fits," she entered a large number (2) beside Accessory to Robbery. "One more to go," she mumbled and looked around to see if anyone heard her. Next the bailiff read:

"Accomplice in a Crime."

"Accomplice in a Crime"—Clisty clicked on that tab. "One who intentionally and voluntarily participates with another in a crime by encouraging or assisting in the commission of the crime or by failing to prevent it though under a duty to do so."

Clisty knew it would be the courts in Illinois that would charge Treadway with fraud, embezzlement of funds, child abuse and whatever else lay incriminating at the bottom of the black valise.

The Allen County Prosecutor, Albert Fisher's opening statements included a reference to Clisty. Her hands froze on the keyboard.

"Ezra Treadway committed kidnapping and criminal confinement of Faith Sterling, and the attempted kidnapping of Clisty Sinclair. These children were only nine years old when this man snatched Faith Sterling out of the Sinclair home, and held Faith from the time she was a nine-years-old child until she was twenty-seven years old. That's eighteen years out of her life! Her parents sit here in the courtroom, praying for justice for their daughter. We are here to see to it their prayers are answered!"

The defense attorney fed the jury lie after lie that Treadway had told them. Ezra Treadway was a master manipulator and he had told his lawyers a believable story that was shot full of holes. It would be the witnesses that would influence the jury though, not the lawyers' rhetoric.

After both the Prosecutor and the defense attorney read their opening statements into the record, Fisher announced. "I'd like to call Melvin Dean Fargo to the stand."

Fargo came in wearing slacks, a sport shirt and sport coat. He was clean shaven and his hair trimmed. It didn't matter how much the Prosecutor's office made him appear to be a respectable citizen, to Clisty, he was still one of the monsters that haunted her nights. She had not seen him the day Treadway nabbed Faith; he was supposed to be waiting in the truck. But, Clisty remembered that she had heard a man's voice at the front door, "Hurry up! I wanna get out of here."

"Mr. Fargo, let the jury know that you have already pleaded guilty to the robbery of Fort Wayne Bank. Is that right?" Fisher questioned.

"Yes," was Fargo's single response.

"Did the Prosecutor's office offer anything to you in exchange for your testimony?"

"Yes."

Treadway sat at the defendant's table, his profile was within Clisty's gaze. She kept her iPad in her lap where she entered data as attorneys began their opening statements. She also began to draw in the sketch pad she had brought. What appeared on the paper was the side view of the man who, to Clisty's mind, personified evil. As she listened to the testimony and mechanically penciled in details of the man—Ezra—she was suddenly aware of all the multitude of frowning, angry lines that filled his face. She decided to finish his sketch later. Flipping the page over, she began to sketch Fargo.

"In your own words," Mr. Fargo, "please tell the jury the terms of the deal you made."

Fargo turned slighted to look at each jury member, and then looked away. "I agreed to testify against Ezra Treadway in exchange for a reduced sentence for bank robbery."

Treadway grabbed the side of the table, growling as he lunged across the surface. "You what?" he roared.

"Mr. Lubansky, please control your defendant," the judge ordered.

"Sorry, Your Honor," Lubansky said as he whispered to Treadway.

"What do you know about the kidnapping of Faith Sterling?" Fisher asked Fargo.

"Ezra and I were having coffee at Mary's Coffee Place on the west side of Chicago, when he started crying. I asked him what was wrong. He said his little girl had just died."

Lubansky stood up, "I object. Your Honor, what does the death of a child have to do with a kidnapping or bank robbery?"

"Mr. Fisher?" Judge Evero raised his eyebrows.

"Mr. Fargo was just about to tell us how all of this connects." Fisher answered then turned back to his witness. "Mr. Treadway was upset over the death of his daughter?"

"Yeah ... yes. He said, his wife—"

"Objection," Lubansky said again, "hearsay."

"Withdraw," Fisher responded. "Mr. Fargo, just tell us how the death of Mr. Treadway's daughter affected you."

"Ezra said his wife was so upset—"

"Your Honor!" Lubansky objected again.

"I'm going to let the witness finish. Then I'll rule if it's admissible," the judge ruled. "Continue Mr. Fargo."

"Ezra asked me to go with him to Indiana to find another daughter for his wife. He said, his grandparents lived in Fort Wayne and he knew his way around."

"Go on," Fisher directed.

"When we got to Fort Wayne, we drove around for a while and finally spotted two girls out exploring alone. We followed them to a house and Treadway waited for a little while to see if he could tell if any adults were at home. He told me to get out and go around and look in the windows while he went to the front door. If I didn't see anyone by the time I got back around to the front, I was to go to the truck and be ready when he came out. I saw him burst through the front door and come out a few minutes later with a girl tucked up under his arm. He threw her in the truck cab between us and we got out of there." Fargo didn't look at Treadway but kept his focus on Fisher.

"Now, can you tell us Treadway's connection to the bank robbery?" Fisher asked.

"When I needed money I'd go over to Naperville, to Ezra's place, and get another payment for keeping my mouth shut about the kidnapping."

"Did you know that Faith Sterling was still held captive in one of the upstairs rooms?"

"I didn't want to know."

"How did Mr. Treadway pay you?" Fisher asked.

"Cash," Fargo said and smiled. "I would only take cash so I didn't have to endorse a check."

"Do you know how much he gave you over the years?" Fisher asked and looked at the jury.

"Ezra knows every penny. He would take a book out of his big safe and write down every dime. I asked him where all that money came from and he said, 'I've got a really good scam going. A little dental work, a haircut and some new clothes is all I needed. The Freedom Temple is as good as Fort Knox.' He said everyone just hands over their money to him."

"Hearsay," Lubansky shouted.

"Don't you worry, Mr. Lubansky," Judge Evero spit back in a well-rehearsed tone. "We'll check all his statements against the facts."

"Do you know of any proof of your statements?" Fisher asked.

"Sure. Treadway loved to count his money over and over. He had it all written down in those books he kept."

"So, each time you went to him, Treadway gave you cash for your silence?" Fisher paced back and forth in front of the witness stand like he was pondering the depth of Treadway's crimes.

"No, not every time. A few times, he said he was getting tired of handing over his money to a taxi driver."

"A taxi driver?" Fisher snapped back.

Fargo stole a glance at Treadway and quickly looked away. "Yeah, because all I did was drive the car. He said he'd planned out some robberies for me to pull to save him his cash."

"Hearsay," Lubansky objected with his hands spread in surrender.

"It's not just my word," Fargo protested. "I saved Ezra's diagrams and instructions."

Fisher took a manila envelope from the defense table and withdrew three pieces of paper. "I would like to enter these into the record as Exhibits A, B, and C." He held up Exhibit A for Fargo to see. "Do you recognize this document?"

"Yes, Sir. That's the first robbery Ezra planned for me."

"Let the jury be aware that experts have analyzed the handwriting and are ready to testify that the handwriting matches Ezra Treadway's," Fisher said and handed the paper to Fargo.

"This paper shows the directions to a hardware store owned by Ezra's uncle, Wade Dunlevy. Ezra said he had spent a summer in Fort Wayne with his grandparents and worked at the Hardware store. The writing says:

1. Payroll in store by Friday noon.

2. Most employees go to lunch between 1 pm and 2 pm. Store traffic down.

3. Money available to cash customer's payroll checks.

4. That cash is in a vault in Dunlevy's office.

5. This last set of numbers is the combination to the vault."

Fargo testified, "I was able to get in the store, ask Dunlevy to find a part I thought would be back in the store room, slip into the office while he was gone, open the safe and was out of there in minutes. I got five-thousand dollars with that job."

Fisher looked at the jury. "So that paper is a complete instruction for the robbery at Dunlevy's Hardware Store," he repeated. "Again, let the jury be aware that all handwriting on the paper belongs to Ezra Treadway. The fingerprints are those of Treadway and Melvin Dean Fargo." He placed the sheet of paper into evidence on the bar of the court.

"What about the robbery at Fort Wayne Bank?" He pulled out another exhibit and showed it to Fargo.

"Yes, those are Ezra's directions to the bank, when to hit it and which teller to approach," Fargo said with growing confidence.

"Why did Treadway identify a specific teller?" Fisher questioned.

"Because, she's his cousin," Fargo pointed accusingly at Treadway. "She had already been through a robbery at the bank before, and Treadway said she was rattled. She had told the family if she was ever held up again, she wouldn't be able to get the money to the robber fast enough and get him out of the bank," Fargo sat back and finally relaxed a little.

Fisher faced the jury and waved the evidence in the air. "Let it be known that the facts of previous robberies and the name of the teller in both cases is indeed the second cousin of Ezra Treadway. All handwriting and fingerprints have been checked and corroborated." Next, Fisher presented Exhibit C. "Tell us about this small piece, Mr. Fargo."

Fargo took the three-by-five card in his hand and flipped it with his fingernail. "This one's old, but I remember it." He squirmed a little in the witness chair and cleared his throat. "See there, at the top, there's a date. The date we drove from Illinois into Fort Wayne, Indiana to snatch Joslyn Treadway."

"Let the court be aware that Joslyn's name at the time of her abduction was Faith Sterling." Then Fisher turned back to the witness. "Go ahead, Mr. Fargo. Tell the court what the rest of the card says."

"It's a list," Fargo explained. "It says:

1. Leave - 9 a.m. sharp
2. Take your gun
3. Gas up the truck – it's a long way to Fort Wayne

That's it. Ezra likes to make lists and keep notes. It makes him seem more in control than others," Fargo added.

"Thank you. I'm finished with this witness," Fisher said.

"You may step down, Mr. Fargo," Judge Evero instructed.

"I would like to call Faith Treadway," Fisher announced.

Once sworn in, Faith sat down, turned and caught Clisty's eye. She smiled faintly and refused to look at Treadway.

"Mrs. Treadway, tell us what happened to you when you were nine years old," Fisher's tone was calm and soothing.

"I was playing at my friend's house, Clisty Sinclair's, when the front door burst open and The Guardian broke in."

"The Guardian?" Fisher questioned. "Is The Guardian here in this courtroom?"

Faith kept her eyes on Fisher, and then turned to the defendant. "That's The Guardian, Ezra Treadway."

"Will you tell the jury why you refer to Treadway as The Guardian?" Fisher asked.

"He kidnapped me and took me to his home in Naperville, Illinois. I never knew his name. I could call him, The Guardian and his wife, Lady. They forced me to live in one of the bedrooms upstairs. I never went outside. No one knew I was there except for Melvin Dean Fargo, but I didn't know his name at the time either. I had a pillowcase over my head part of the way to Illinois and only got a few glimpses of Fargo."

Faith was on the witness stand for a long time. Then, Lubansky cross examined her.

"Mrs. Treadway, Ezra Treadway is your father-in-law isn't he?" Lubansky asked with hostility in his voice.

"Yes, I guess he is."

"You guess? Are you that confused?"

Fisher jumped up. "Your Honor, I object to the tone Mr. Lubansky is using. Faith has been through enough."

"I'm sorry," Lubansky apologized, and then turned back to her. "If you're going to accuse a man of something, he has a right to face you." His voice rose and grew louder. "Take another look at the defendant. Can't you face him?"

"Yes!" Faith hissed as she turned. "I can look at him, even though I was his child-slave, a phantom in his presence. He rarely talked to me except to yell and berate me. He never touched me except to beat me or slap me across the room, just as he did my daughter, his loving granddaughter, recently. I was a prisoner in his home. I never went to school or to the church he was the so-called Spiritual Leader in." Her eyes flared and her cheeks grew red with anger. She stuck out her finger the full length of her arm. "There's the man, my kidnapper, the man who illegally confined me for eighteen years and ... the guardian of ... nothing," she yelled and stared Treadway down.

The people in the courtroom whispered between one another. "He's evil," one of them said. "I'd like to get my hands on him," a man muttered. The judge pounded the gavel on the strike plate, gaveling the room to silence.

"I have no more questions of this witness," the defense attorney stated.

Faith stood up and waited for a few seconds while the anger, that had set her body shaking, settled down. She said nothing but held her head high and stared at Treadway as she walked passed him, touched Clisty on the shoulder as she passed and walked out of the courtroom.

"Would Mrs. Emily Treadway come to the stand?" Fisher called.

"What?" Lubansky jumped to his feet. "Side bar, please."

Fisher and Lubansky came to the well of the court. "A woman cannot be forced to testify against her husband," Lubansky protested.

"She isn't being forced, Your Honor. And her words are not to accuse Ezra Treadway as much as they are to validate Faith Treadway's testimony. Since Ezra would not allow anyone else in the house and Faith wasn't permitted to go anywhere, Mrs. Emily Treadway, Faith's little daughter Pooky, and Faith's husband, who is now deceased, are the only people who could testify to her existence for the last eighteen years."

Judge Evero ground his teeth and shot a side glance to Ezra. "If it is Mrs. Treadway's desire to speak, I am certainly not going to stop her. Let the record state that she is not required to testify, however."

Emily Treadway came to the witness stand for swearing in. Her long hair, swept back from its peasant style, was fashioned into a soft cluster of curls gathered into a loose bun. As she sat down, the judge addressed her. "Mrs. Treadway, I need to ask you again if you have been forced or coerced into testifying against your husband, Ezra Treadway."

"I was not coerced at all," she said with her head held high and defiance in her whisper-soft voice. She locked eyes with Ezra and did not release him from her gaze.

Treadway's face grew hard and dark. His brows furrowed with deep menacing lines. Emily's expression was defiant in the face of his silent intimidation.

"Tell me why you volunteered to testify today, Mrs. Treadway," Fisher asked. He stood back from the witness stand. Both the jury and Ezra Treadway himself were within her gaze.

"I must testify to the presence of a wonderful child and beautiful daughter in my home. No one ever saw her ..." she started to sob and then swallowed hard, regaining her voice. "But, I have to let everyone know she was there, hidden away, in our upstairs." She looked at Ezra and snapped. "That hateful man, Ezra Treadway, brought Faith into our home, saying that he had adopted her in Indiana. He named her Joselyn and she never heard the name Faith again. In fact, Ezra never told her what her new last name was, Treadway. But, I'll have to admit, once Joselyn came out of the shock of having been ripped from her home and parents ... she told me something." She looked back at Roma and Ralph. They were crying.

"Joselyn did tell me that she had a mom and dad and that her name was Faith. I thought, or I wanted to think, that Jocelyn was just wishful-thinking, that she hadn't gotten over the grief from the death of both of her parents. That's what Ezra had told me." Emily blew her nose and wiped tears from her eyes.

She continued. "Joselyn was a good girl, an inquisitive and smart girl. But, if she spoke up about anything ... that she didn't like cauliflower for supper, Ezra would hit her, or even beat her. She was a prisoner in our home. Ezra called her his slave-child. A few times he told her that her parents didn't die, that they had sold her to him. I cried myself to sleep many nights."

"Why didn't you protect her or get her out of there?" Fisher asked.

"I tried a couple of times. I was beaten and, one time, he twisted my arm until it broke. He told me, if I ever attempted to run away with Joselyn, he would throw me out and keep Joselyn ... if I tried anything. Our own son, Steven, who became Faith's husband and Pooky's father, could not stand up to him. If Steven said anything to anyone, his schooling would stop and he wouldn't be able to go anywhere. I had to get Ezra's permission to leave the house every time, or even go out in the yard. I had no car. I didn't know how to drive." She cleared her throat and whispered. "Really, I guess we were all held captive by Ezra Treadway."

Emily sipped from a glass of water the Prosecutor provided, and then handed it back. "Ezra wouldn't let me call the doctor when Steven had a heart attack ... he was so young. Ezra said no one was coming in the house. He said, all we had to do was pray and if Steven died, it was our fault because we didn't pray hard enough."

"Were you at fault, Mrs. Treadway?" Fisher asked. "Did Steven die because you and Faith didn't pray hard enough?"

"Of course not," Emily stated with a small measure of confidence. "God has plans beyond anything we can understand. It was only because Steven died, and Ezra and I were at the funeral, that Joselyn and Pooky were alone in the house for a few hours. God used Steven's death to free Faith and my dear granddaughter. They were able to escape, even though I couldn't set them free." She straightened her back and glared at Ezra Treadway.

The court buzzed again with whispers and tears. The judge did nothing to silence the room. Lubansky sat at the defense table and flipped his pen back and forth in his fingertips, silent.

"I have no questions for this witness," Lubansky said boldly. Treadway seethed, with his shoulders raised, like a mad dog, ready to attack. Lubansky didn't even look at him.

Part VI
Justice Served - 1

After days of testimony, the jury finally retired to deliberate. Clisty didn't report the daily account of the events in court. She didn't want any reason for Ezra to have a retrial. There would be time for all of that when the Network wound up filming the whole story. They decided to release her sketches during that evening's news. She walked out to the outer hall and stretched, trying to work the anger out of her body that had been stored in her muscles since she was nine.

"I'm here for you, Babe," Jake said as he came up behind her and rubbed her back. "All we can do now is to wait for the jury to come in."

"I know," Clisty said as she turned. She lifted Jake's right arm and threw it over her shoulder and the same with his left. Smiling up at him she surrendered to his safe embrace. "It's been so long. How will I ever do a story every week?"

"You do it all the time now," Jake encouraged her. "There's something new on each broadcast, Hon. Every evening you report a new account of the happenings and people of Fort Wayne."

"I know. I guess it's still the geography that has me rattled." She buried her head in Jake's shoulder and sighed. "It's this case, having Faith back and at the same time, I have to make a major decision about my career."

"Is the network still waiting for your answer to their New York offer?" he asked.

"Yeah," she sighed. "They said, after the trial they'll want an answer. The trial will be over soon. Now, I'm too tired to think about any of it."

"Clisty, this story will be far different from all the others you will cover and far more difficult. This one is as personal as it gets. Treadway kidnapped your best friend right out of your own living room and he nearly took you too. He had his hands on you until you got away and he jerked Faith right out of your grasp. He touched you as much as he touched Faith that day. You are emotionally exhausted, which is a lot harder than physical exhaustion." Jake soothed her back with gentle hands.

"You're right, Jake. I know you're right," Clisty whispered as she remained in his arms. "I can't ignore how angry, afraid, weak, vulnerable, and happy I've felt through all of this. Happy, obviously, because I'm glad Faith is home. But, the other stuff, the bad feelings, sometimes, I experience all of those emotions at the same time!"

They clustered in the hall for as long as it took for all four of them to gather, Clisty and Jake, Becca and Clint. Then the Sterlings came out of the courtroom. Clisty put her arms around Roma and kissed her cheek. "Are you two holding up okay? We're going to film some comments. Can we hear from you two?"

"From Ralph, maybe. I have nothing to say right now," Roma said. "I am so upset. That man is a monster and his wife was so weak, she went along with his demands."

"I understand," Clisty empathized with her. "How is Faith doing?"

"She's at home, but I don't want the TV audience to know where she is. She's alone. I'm still terrified for them both. We're going to hurry home to be with her," Mrs. Sterling whispered. Then she smiled and her voice cracked. "Faith held Pooky out of school until the trial was over. My sweet granddaughter went off to school today—her first day in a new school, in any school for that matter."

She brushed a tear from her cheek. "Pooky was so excited. It's a new beginning for all of us."

"Sorry to break this up, Mrs. Sterling," Becca chimed in softly. "I don't want to rush any of you, but I think we'd better get some video while we're here outside the courtroom. It's always good to get immediate reactions if at all possible. We'll use it for the eleven o'clock news or save it for the News Magazine. We'll look at all of it and then decide."

Clint stepped back from the small cluster gathered around Clisty. With the TV camera in his hand, he quickly found a good spot, raised the camera, adjusted the lens and started filming. Becca stepped behind him, out of the shot, where she could see what he saw in the view finder. She paused for only a second and then made the thumbs up gesture. She put up three fingers, counting down to zero. Clisty knew they were ready.

"We are outside the courtroom where the jury has just received instructions from the judge. They will not be back until they have reached a verdict." She looked over and nodded toward Roma and Ralph as they stood just beyond the view of the camera. "Mr. and Mrs. Sterling, is there anything you would like our audience to know?"

Ralph took Roma by the elbow and led her over to the microphone. Ralph began. "We are hopeful that justice will be served. Treadway took our daughter's childhood away from her and our lives away from us at the same time. I want him punished. Mrs. Treadway's testimony told us that someone in that house loved Faith. I know that no one ever expressed it, but we hope Faith felt it. For that, we will be eternally grateful. Pooky, our granddaughter, loves Emily Treadway and that tells us there was love in their house in spite of that ... man. We will wait for the jury's verdict. In fact," he looked at his watch. "We're going home to get Faith and we'll all be right back, in case the jury doesn't deliberate for very long. Then, we'll play it hour by hour, day by day, just like we have lived for eighteen years, until this nightmare is over."

"Thank you;" Clisty said. "We know what this trial has meant to all of you. This is Clisty Sinclair for the News at Eleven." The microphone suddenly felt heavy in her hands. She handed it to Clint.

"Let's all go for some supper," Clisty said. "Mr. Fisher has our cell phone numbers and will call us when the verdict comes in. Maybe a little food will give us the energy to get through this."

"Perfect," Becca agreed.

"If we go to the Courtroom Grill across the street, we won't have far to come back if the verdict comes in fast," Jake offered.

"During supper?" Becca quipped. "We should eat at the train station if Treadway is on the fast track to the pen."

"I think I could eat an entire Thanksgiving feast in the few minutes we'll be gone," Clisty said as she allowed herself to pay attention to her body. "I had no idea I was hungry until now."

VI

Justice Served - 2

"The restaurant seems miles away," Clisty said as they hustled down the limestone steps and across the street. They paused and waited for a minute at the door for Clint to stow the camera in the news van and lock up before going in to order. "This is nerve-wracking for me," Clisty added.

"You've been through a lot," Becca reminded her.

"Becca, we all have," Clisty protested. "I'm no different than the rest of you. We all went to Illinois."

"Clisty, he attacked you, too," Becca reminded her. "It seems like you don't believe you have a right to be upset over all of this. You and Faith were inseparable as children. He stalked you both. He broke in on you both. He grabbed you both and dragged you both across the floor. You now have survivor's guilt that you had gotten away. No, Clisty, you have a right to acknowledge your own feelings," Becca said as Clint came over from the van. "Remember, Treadway also showed up at Roma and Ralph's house and threatened you all with a Glock 27!"

"Becca's right this time, Hon," Jake joined in. "The difference between you and Faith is where and how you've lived these last eighteen years, but there's no difference in the events of the kidnapping. You were both attacked by a very dangerous man." He placed his hand on Clisty's shoulder and massaged in a generous measure of his love.

Clint hurried across the street, pulled on the door handle and stepped back. "You guys haven't gotten a table for us yet?"

"Just waitin' for you," Becca said as she zipped past him.

They stepped inside where others appeared to have the same idea. The packed grill was full of many of the same faces Clisty had seen in the courtroom. The four of them managed to find the last table in the place and settled in to order. Luckily, it was in the far back corner of the dining room. There would be a small measure of privacy, away from the hubbub.

"Do you know what you want, or do you need a menu?" a waitress asked as they all settled and removed their jackets.

"I'll have soup and coffee," Clisty said. "The soup is already prepared," she reminded the others. "I won't have to wait for it to be cooked. I want food. I don't care about fine dining right now. It'll be scooped and served."

"What kind?" the waitress asked.

"Potato rivel," Clisty said and placed her napkin in her lap like she had just made a major decision. "Be sure to stir the soup up from the bottom real good. Don't just ladle it from the top of the pot. I like plenty of potatoes and a ton of rivels. I'll add my own pepper." Then she noticed the others watching her. "What?" she laughed. "I know what I want and I know how I want it served. Deal with it," she laughed again. "I'm too tired to eat, but hungry. Potatoes with rivels may hit the spot."

"Make mine the same," Jake echoed. "I even like the description of how I want it put in the bowl, but I would have no way of repeating the instructions."

Becca and Clint each raised their index finger, a silent affirmation to order the soup and coffee. Becca made a stirring gesture and then a dipping motion into an imaginary bowl. "I'm sure you get the idea," she mouthed as she yawned.

Clint just pointed at Becca, Jake and Clisty, then nodded and pointed to himself.

"Got ya," the waitress said as she wrote on her order pad, "Soup, soup, soup and soup." Then she walked away.

The coffee came first and they each sipped in silence. Clisty looked at all of her tired friends as their shoulders slumped and they stared into their cups. She chose not to use the window as a mirror. Whatever she looked like, she knew she was still awake and that alone was an accomplishment.

"Will I ever feel rested again," Clisty sighed deeply.

"Four bowls of soup," the waitress announced as she placed them in front of each one. Then she added, "Please notice all the potatoes and rivels. I'll be happy to receive a generous tip, equal to the number of potatoes you can count." She winked and walked away.

"This looks good," Jake inhaled the steam as it rose from the bowl. "It smells great too."

"Grandma makes rivel soup," Clisty thought out loud. "I like to mix the rivels with my hands and drop them, little by little, into the potato soup."

"What exactly is a rivel?" Clint asked as he didn't hesitate for a moment. He stuck his spoon in the soup over and over, while wearing a grin on his face.

"Rivels are like dumpling dough," Clisty answered. "Only you don't roll it out. You mix it by hand and drop it into the soup a little at a time, crumbling the dough with your fingers as you release it."

Then, Clisty's mind drifted to the dear ones. "My grandparents came home from Florida last week, in time to get regular updates on the case. Grandma kept saying, 'It could have been you too, Clisty.' She told me she has prayed for me every day of my life and twice a day since the trial started. She even bought a new prayer angel to replace the one she lost." Clisty ate a few bites of rivels and potatoes and added, "She said the angel's face looked like me. I could sure feel those prayers."

"I know; me too," Becca agreed in a sleepy tone.

"I think this soup was made by angels," Jake added.

Clint didn't look up from his bowl. "I don't care who made it."

They finished their meal and were just discussing the merits of sugar cream pie, the pie of Indiana, as opposed to fruit pie when Clisty's phone vibrated on the table, setting off a clatter of spoons.

"All ready?" Clisty stared at her cell phone.

"I'll throw down thirty dollars; that'll cover us all plus a good tip. Let's get back over there," Jake offered.

They gathered up all their belongings. Clisty, Jake and Becca hurried ahead, while Clint got the camera from the van. While he couldn't film inside the courtroom, it had to be ready to aim and focus at the point of Becca's finger.

Across the street, up the steps and through the double doors, the three hurried inside and slipped into their seats, just as the bailiff announced, "All rise." Faith and her parents darted in as the courtroom doors started to close and took seats behind Clisty and all.

Jury members entered quietly with bowed heads. None of them looked at Treadway. Clisty thought that might be a sign of victory for Faith and whispered a little prayer that justice would be served. The jury took their seats in heavy silence. The only sound was the squeak of chairs and Roma's whispered prayer as she clutched Faith's hand.

Clisty flipped open her sketch pad and pulled a pencil from her bag. The lead flew over the thick paper as she blocked in every juror, their body posture and a suggestion of the tortured emotion that registered on each one's face. She wondered what it would be like to sit in judgment over someone else. Then, she realized she had pronounced Ezra Treadway guilty every day of her life, she just didn't know his name.

"The jury has indicated they have reached a verdict." Judge Evero said. "Will the Foreperson hand the verdict to the bailiff?"

The bailiff walked over to the foreperson, collected the verdict slip and delivered the piece of paper to the judge. Evero opened it, read it and handed it back to the bailiff. The defendant and his lawyer stood.

The bailiff read, "To the count of Criminal Confinement, the verdict is … guilty."

Mumbled voices of relieve and expelled tension were heard all over the court. The judge just looked at the people and waited for silence again. Then he nodded to the bailiff.

"To the charge of Accessory to Robbery, the verdict is … guilty."

The room stirred again but the bailiff continued. "To the charge of Accomplice in a Crime, the verdict is … guilty."

Judge Evero gaveled the court and then added, "Sentencing will be four weeks from today. I'd like to thank the jury for your time." He gaveled again.

"Court is adjourned," the bailiff announced.

Ezra Treadway turned and glared at Clisty. "I should have taken you, too," he growled. "I would've taught you to keep your mouth shut."

Lubansky said something to Treadway in obvious anger. Armed guards pulled Treadway away. While being led from the courtroom, he yelled, "I would have broken you!"

Clisty stared at the man of evil, her head held high and her eyes fixed on his in righteous defiance, until he was completely out of the courtroom. Then, she turned her back for a moment, and smiled. To Jake, she whispered, "After eighteen years, he couldn't break Faith Sterling. Why did he think he could break me?"

"I would place my bet on you any day, tough lady," Jake said as he laughed.

Still in the courtroom, Faith hurried over to Clisty, smiling a real smile for the first time in, maybe, eighteen years, Clisty guessed. "Thank you, thank you so much," Faith repeated as she clung to

Clisty. "You saw me when no one had seen me for eighteen years, and you remembered."

Clisty wiped tears from her face as she spoke softly in Faith's ear. "You have been in my thoughts every day since you were taken. I could never forget those beautiful, friendly eyes. I looked for them everywhere I went." Stepping back, she studied her friend's face. "Would you like to be on camera and give the world your immediate reaction to the verdict?"

Faith looked over at her parents but didn't hesitate, "Yes, I would. I've waited a long time to speak openly with no fear of punishment. Now is the time."

VI

Justice Served - 3

Out in the hall, Clisty noticed a man in a black business suit standing off to the side, watching her prepare to interview. She didn't recognize the on-looker as one of those who frequently waited outside the courtroom during the trial. She put curiosity aside, focused on her job and held the microphone out to Jake. "Detective Jake Davis, if you have time, can you give our viewers your reaction to the jury's decision?"

Jake moved in close to Clisty. "I think it's great, and I'm sure we're all happy that the verdict came in so fast. That was especially good for all those affected by Ezra Treadway's actions. Sometimes, trials drag on for months and the deliberations stretch on and on some more. That re-inflicts additional pain on the victims involved, as they sit every day in the courtroom and see the evil face of the one who harmed them. The brave people in this trial didn't have to wait." He paused, looked into the camera lens and pronounced with certainty, "And, justice was served."

"Thank you Detective," Clisty said. Jake touched her hand as he stepped away. When the door swung open and Faith came out, Clisty caught her eye and smiled. Faith walked over, within the interview circle.

"As you know," Clisty said as she spoke into the camera, "this is Faith Sterling Treadway, the woman who was kidnapped as a child, and held in an upstairs room in Illinois for eighteen years. Most of us would demand the most severe punishment for all those involved." She turned to her friend, "Is there anything you would like to say to our news audience, Mrs. Treadway?"

Faith embraced her friend. "Thank you, Clisty." She reached for the microphone as her brows started to knit together. She cleared her throat and seemed to try to relax her expression along with her emotions. With her hand to her face, she whispered. "I want everyone to know, Clisty, you looked for me when I could only leave a tiny clue that I was back. You remembered enough of the little girl who was lost for so long, that you recognized a frightened woman when she returned." Faith struggled with tears that caught in her throat. "My parents are wonderful and have pledged to help my daughter and me for as long as we need their help. We will always need their love." She stopped when Emily Treadway came out into the hall. Faith didn't flinch, but reached out and put her arm around the woman. "Come over here, Emily," she said as she squeezed Emily's shoulder. "I have to let the viewers know, my daughter finally has a real second grandmother. Emily was as much a victim of Ezra Treadway as I was, as my husband, Steven was, too." She kissed Emily's cheek. "I know, when Emily's spirit heals, she and Pooky will enjoy many good times together. My parents have told her she is welcome to visit in their home." Faith kissed Emily again as the woman sobbed.

"I …" Emily tried to speak. She looked up at Faith and patted her on the face. "I know you are Faith Sterling, but you will always be my Joselyn. I love you … and I vow to never use that name again. I am so sorry for everything, Faith" she said as her whole body slumped in emotional pain as she walked on.

Faith looked at the camera and continued. "Today is about justice being served. Some will never receive justice equal to the crimes that have been committed against them. I don't know yet how many years Ezra Treadway will be in prison, but eighteen years would not be too many for me. The man was depraved-evil at the door, not the guardian at the gate" Then she clutched the microphone, her knuckles taunt and her jaw set, "And, that man needs to know … I am not broken, nor am I silent. I will speak out against emotional and physical abuse any time it rears its ugly head. Today, its ugly head has just been found guilty!"

Clisty put her arm around Faith and gave her a sideways hug. "Anytime you need a really big voice to share your message of love over abuse, Faith, you have a platform at WFT-TV."

Faith hugged Clisty again as the Sterlings came into the hall. They met up at the microphone. "We are leaving our sorrow and anger right here," Ralph said. "We're going home now to celebrate family."

The camera lights went out and all was silent for a moment. "That was wonderful, Clisty," Becca said softly. "That will be great footage during the late night news. But, it's more than that; it was the right story to pursue."

VI

Justice Served - 4

Clisty turned around and looked for Jake, assuming he was still in the courthouse. The hour was late. He had taken personal time off from the police department to be with her during the trial, so he wasn't on duty. He didn't have to report in, but she didn't see him anywhere.

"Have you seen Jake?" Clisty asked Clint as she helped him collect his camera gear.

"No," he said off handed and then added, "oh, wait. He said he had talked to someone here in the hall and thought he'd better check in at police headquarters. He said he'll meet you at the TV station after the eleven o'clock news."

She looked toward the door, half expecting to see him wave on his way out. He was nowhere. He left without saying anything—Jake was gone. Who did he talk to? Why did the conversation cause him to leave?

"Clisty Sinclair," the man in the suit, with a portfolio under his arm, reached out his hand in greeting. He was impeccably dressed in dark suit, black shirt and tie.

"Yes," she acknowledged as she continued to look beyond the doors. Turning back to the suit man, she apologized. "I'm sorry. I was looking for Detective Davis just as you came up." She tilted her head a little, puzzled, and asked, "Is there something I can do for you?"

"I was talking to Davis while you were helping your camera man pack the equipment. The detective was very interested in your career," the man offered with open arms, then clapped them together—the non-verbal message? All is settled.

"You talked to him?" Clisty wasn't sure she liked that. A total stranger was discussing her career with Jake. "Who did you say you are? What can I do for you?"

"We are hoping there is something we can do for you, Miss Sinclair." He pulled a business card from his inner jacket pocket and handed it to her. "I'm Victor Rogers, Vice President of the network ... your network."

Clisty's mouth dropped open; she covered it with her hand. "Mr. Rogers," she stammered and shook his hand again. "I am so sorry. I had no idea a representative of the network was in town. Did you see the remote filming?"

"Yes, we are very interested in your work. Bradley Funderbird had spoken to you on the phone, but he wanted me to come to Indiana to talk to you in person. He has an amended offer he wants me to go over with you."

"Funderbird?" Becca asked as she walked closer. "I've heard that name before."

"Yes, you have," Clisty said. "When he called the first time, I talked to you about him. He's the president of the network," she said as she studied Becca's expression. Maybe her friend would be able to help her find the answers she needed.

"From what I've seen, Brad has found another star ... in you, Clisty." Rogers picked up her hand and shook it, affirming her work. Recognition from New York was pretty heady stuff for an Indiana girl.

"Thank you." She looked at Becca, hoping to get a clue of what was going on inside her head. She turned back to Rogers, "You said, 'an amended offer.' What does that mean?"

"Mr. Funderbird is sensing that you may not want to actually move to New York permanently. So, he is proposing a change in logistics. Your research team will be in New York. They will email all the information to you here in Fort Wayne. Obviously, you will have to go to the mid-western town in which your story takes place and spend a day filming, interviewing, gathering videos, regardless of where your base is. You'll write your interview questions and finished story in an office right here in Fort Wayne and email it all to New York. You'll electronically send all video to the network office. They'll edit it and prepare it for viewing during the weekly News Magazine. You can even choose your own film crew and back-up team, local researcher and secretary." He looked at Becca and Clint. "You can film your segment from the studio right here in Fort Wayne. There may be an occasional reason why you would need to go to New York, but we'll arrange plenty of time for Broadway plays and shopping while you're there."

Clisty looked at Becca who was near the bursting point then back at Rogers "That sounds wonderful. But … there's another person I want to talk to first."

"Clisty!" Becca burst out.

Clisty waved her hand in measured beats. "It's okay, Becca, but I really want to run all of this by someone else, before I make a major change. I like the feeling that there are other people in my life and I want to respect that."

"Your agent and attorney?" Rogers guessed. "We'll be happy to forward all contracts and agreements to them. You should have professionals look over the paperwork. But it's your decision—it's all up to you. Miss Sinclair, I'd say you're the one holding the microphone this time."

Clisty and Becca hugged and jumped up and down. Stoic Clint smiled broadly and did his own version of jumping, within the limits of his earth-bound feet.

"We all get a huge career boost," Becca squealed.

"That's wonderful … but it sure puts increased tension on my decision," Clisty frowned.

Becca looked at her in disbelief. "You mean, with all that the network is offering, it still doesn't guarantee a 'yes' from you?" Her voice sounded irritated.

"I love everything I hear from the network," Clisty turned back to Rogers. "I really do. I just want to talk to Jake first." She resisted the urge to answer without honoring the growing relationship she had with Jake. She wanted to say "yes, of course," but would her disregard of Jake's feelings and opinion harm their relationship? "That doesn't mean I'll let Jake answer for me." She turned back to Becca. "You know me better than that." She raised both hands in a gesture of finality. "I just don't want him to hear about the job after I have already decided."

"Fantastic," Rogers looked up to the ceiling in relief. "I trust you Clisty Sinclair. If I didn't, I wouldn't offer you a contract ... and here it is." He handed her the portfolio he had carried. "Take it to your attorney and either mail it back as quickly as you can, or hand-carry it to New York. The News Magazine team would love to meet you."

"I like the last idea," Clisty said as she smiled. Thoughts of New York in the spring fluttered through her head like butterflies around pastel colored flowers in a Central Park garden. The City could be magical.

"Just one more thing," Rogers began.

"Oh no, here it comes," Becca jibed.

"No changes from the offer." Rogers threw up his hand like he was taking an oath and laughed.

"Then what?" Clisty asked.

"Mr. Funderbird would like you to use the new signoff tonight on your news program as you wind up Ezra Treadway's segment."

Clisty stopped for a moment. "I will, if it's okay with my station boss, the General Manager. I haven't even told him about this promotion." She thumped her finger tips to her forehead. "Good grief. I'll have to give notice."

"Mr. Funderbird will take care of that. He'll make sure the stories you cover in the first two months of the News Magazine are as near to the Fort Wayne area as possible. That way you can still do the local news, at least the late edition. The Fort Wayne station will have two months to find your replacement and you'll be able to transition slowly and smoothly."

"You'll be busy, Clisty," Becca acknowledged, and encouraged her, "but you can do it ... if you really want to."

"It sounds doable," Clisty clapped her hands together, a small attempt to cheer herself on.

"Here is the sign-off for tonight's news," Rogers said as he handed her a piece of paper. He pointed to the portfolio. "And, your contract, have it read by professionals." He patted her arm and smiled. "I'll leave you now. I have just enough time to make my flight." He took her hand again. "We will connect from New York for your eleven o'clock news using the online link from your station's website. We all hope to hear the new sign-off. Then we'll know we will see you in New York soon." He turned and walked quickly toward the door and waved.

"Yes, yes!" Clisty sang out with excitement.

"Clisty, I cannot believe it! I'm so excited I could bust!" Becca waved her arms around in the air, celebrating. Then she grabbed hold of Clisty's sleeve and pulled. "Why are you hesitating? Jake has no say in your job."

"I know that," she stated firmly. "He has no right to tell me what to do and I'm not going to let him. I just want him to be part of the excitement, not a bystander to a parade he wasn't invited to join."

"Well, okay," Becca agreed as she checked the large clock on the wall. "Hey, we'd better move, too. Clint and I will drop you off at your place so you can rest before the eleven o'clock news. I'll pick you up later and take you to the station for the broadcast since your car is already there. Dan can handle the early evening edition solo."

Clisty threw her head back and laughed. "He'll be happy about that. He seems to be feeling left out lately." Clisty's smile grew as she walked toward the door, aware she was walking into a great adventure.

"I wonder how Dan will take the news of your promotion," Clint added.

"I don't even want to think about that now," Clisty shuddered, "except to say, I don't want anyone to brag or talk to him in a superior tone. It was Faith Sterling's resurrection from the dead, not anything we did, that gave us this opportunity. We just followed the story and brought her home."

• • • • •

"I'm glad you got here before air time," Clisty said breathlessly as Jake came into the station. "I got ready for the broadcast and have been watching for you."

"I'm here. This sounds serious, Clisty," his face grew sober as he planted both feet firmly on the tile floor.

"It is," she ran her fingers down the front of his jacket. "It's good news for me."

"Then, is it good news for me, too?"

"Jake, I can't be one of those women who give up their identity to be absorbed by the man in her life." She looked up and met his eyes. "I cannot walk behind you, and I have no desire to walk ahead of you. If we can't walk together, side-by-side ... we can't walk at all."

"Now wait a minute, Clisty." His face did not change to anger or defensiveness. But, his point was clear and loving. "I can't be one of those guys who are so insecure that they have to force the woman in their life to give up who she is to be with him. I want you to walk beside me, Clisty. I depend on you and you depend on me, out of love, not out of coercion. We are perfectly capable of depending on ourselves." He smiled and put his arms around her, picking her up completely off the floor. "It is just so much more fun being with you, than always being the lone wolf of Fort Wayne. I have you and you have me."

"You definitely have me," Clisty assured him. "She pulled close and their kiss was warm and tender. Then she added, "I just happen to also have a great job that I'm really going to enjoy."

"Oh no," Becca moaned. "Don't mess up your make-up."

"I'm fine, Becca," Clisty said as she nuzzled her head in Jake's chest and laughed.

"So, by all the display of affection, I assume she told you about our promotions," she bubbled.

"Becca," Clisty scolded as she stood back. "You're rushing things."

"No," Jake replied. "I just know I want what Clisty wants."

"Oh great," Becca teased, "then having Fort Wayne as her base, not New York, choosing Clint and me as her local *and* network team, hiring a researcher and secretary, and going to New York every once in a while, mostly to play, are just unimportant details of the job?"

"Oh, thank goodness," Jake sighed loudly, threw both arms up and seemed to go weak-kneed. "Praise the Lord!"

"Yeah, right, you just wanted what Clisty wanted all along." Becca rolled her eyes and laughed.

"I understand, Jake," Clisty agreed as she pretended to prop him up. "I have been feeling the same way! It had to work out for both of us or it couldn't work at all."

"Come on, Clisty," Becca urged. "No time for all of that." She took her by the arm and coaxed her away from Jake. "You'd better get used to rushing about, at least for the next few months," she directed Clisty toward the studio. ""It's almost time for the news."

Clisty, Becca and Clint went into the studio and Jake watched from the studio window. It would be the local wrap-up of Faith's story. The network story would be weeks away. They took their places and Dan Drummond slid onto the first anchor seat.

"You've had quite a day … actually, quite a week," Dan acknowledged. His friendly tone was a relief to Clisty. The lights went on and they began.

The newscast that night had progressed through the local high school sports scores and the weather for the area. Dan Drummond reported on a three car pile-up on I-469 near exit 25, with the help of a film crew that provided video from the site.

Clisty gave her report of the trial of Ezra Treadway, including the video filmed after the verdict came in. There was a minute left in the broadcast. Clisty had pre-read the announcement the network had given her many times, so she was prepared.

"The rest of Faith Sterling Treadway's story is being edited and will comprise a segment for the Network News Magazine I've been asked to participate in." She smiled with excitement into the camera. "In future programs we may follow another thread in Faith's story, her experience in Illinois. Will our neighboring state bring additional charges against Ezra Treadway?"

Becca crossed her fingers behind the camera. Would Clisty make it official? Would she say the words Funderbird had written— the words that would promote them all? On the other side of the glass, Jake smiled a knowing smile.

"That is the News at Eleven. We thank you all for watching. Your interest in the lives of those in northeast Indiana, and in my dear childhood friend, Faith, is what makes our newscasts a success. Some laughingly call the Midwest, fly-over country, implying that the only news of value happens on the two coasts. We know that isn't true and our network has affirmed it. The Heartland, everything in the middle of America, is just that, the very heart of our great country. Beginning tonight, the President of the network has asked me to give special reports on each of the Network Weekly News Magazine programs. I'm signing off tonight with the closing signature for each of my contributions to that program." She took a breath and relaxed. "This is Clisty Sinclair, with *Stories from the Heartland.*"

Other Books by Doris Gaines Rapp

Novels:
Length of Days – The Age of Silence (1st in the trilogy)
Length of Days – Beyond the Valley of the Keepers (2nd in the trilogy)
Hiawassee – Child of the Meadow
Smoke from Distant Fires
Escape from the Belfry

Non-Fiction:
Prayer Therapy of Jesus
Promote Yourself
Waiting for Jesus in a Can't Wait World – Advent 2014

Post-to-Phone Messages
Prayer for Release of Anxiety

Collection:
Christmas Feather, one of eight short stories in a wonderful collection titled,
Christmases Past

Children's:
Lincoln's Christmas Mouse

Internet Presence

Facebook: Doris Gaines Rapp – Author Page
www.dorisgainesrapp.blogspot.com
www.prayertherapyrapp.blogspot.com
www.dorisgainesrapp.com
www.lengthofdays.net

dorisgainesrapp@gmail.com